"Don't think you [can get?] away with this indefinitely, Goldilocks," he murmured,

"because I know what you're up to." He raised his head and cupped her chin with his hand, tilting her face toward his. "You've been trying to distract me, but you're only postponing the inevitable. Eventually, you'll have to listen to the truth—"

"Hush, darling." She pulled his head down to hers and silenced him with a kiss. She had already tossed his necktie to the far end of the sofa and now she began unbuttoning his shirt. He inhaled raggedly at the tantalizing brush of her hands upon his skin, and his arms clamped around her possessively.

"You win, Darcy," he growled. "This time we'll do it your way—but only because I want you too damned much to argue about it."

He hugged her to him with breathtaking ardor and his mouth came down on hers in a plundering, ravishing kiss. Both of them were writhing, straining to be even closer, and for a blissful time arguments were forgotten.

Dear Reader:

As the months go by, we continue to receive word from you that SECOND CHANCE AT LOVE romances are providing you with the kind of romantic entertainment you're looking for. In your letters you've voiced enthusiastic support for SECOND CHANCE AT LOVE, you've shared your thoughts on how personally meaningful the books are, and you've suggested ideas and changes for future books. Although we can't always reply to your letters as quickly as we'd like, please be assured that we appreciate your comments. Your thoughts are all-important to us!

We're glad many of you have come to associate SECOND CHANCE AT LOVE books with our butterfly trademark. We think the butterfly is a perfect symbol of the reaffirmation of life and thrilling new love that SECOND CHANCE AT LOVE heroines and heroes find together in each story. We hope you keep asking for the "butterfly books," and that, when you buy one—whether by a favorite author or a talented new writer—you're sure of a good read. You can trust all SECOND CHANCE AT LOVE books to live up to the high standards of romantic fiction you've come to expect.

So happy reading, and keep your letters coming!

With warm wishes,

Ellen Edwards

Ellen Edwards
SECOND CHANCE AT LOVE
The Berkley/Jove Publishing Group
200 Madison Avenue
New York, NY 10016

P. S. Everyone at SECOND CHANCE AT LOVE wishes you a *very* romantic Valentine's Day.

BELOVED STRANGER
MICHELLE ROLAND

A
SECOND CHANCE AT LOVE
BOOK

BELOVED STRANGER

Chapter 1

ON THE DAY she received her final decree in the mail, Darcy Cummins did a number of things the experts in such matters advise a recently divorced person not to do.

First she dug her wedding album out of the storage locker in the basement of her apartment building. Then she put her Dionne Warwick recording of "I'll Never Love This Way Again" on the stereo and played it time after time while she looked through the album, studying the photographs of Tim until his smooth, handsome face was sharply etched in her mind.

And that night, she almost went to bed with a perfect stranger.

This came about because she made a dinner reservation at the little Italian restaurant Tim and she had discovered when they were newlyweds and still in love. She hadn't been to Santino's for nearly two years, but the maître d' remembered her. He automatically led her to the table by the windows that she and Tim had always preferred.

After she'd placed her order, Darcy nibbled on the breadsticks and watched as the lights of Seattle winked on. She soaked up the romantic atmosphere of the restaurant, attempting to recapture the time when she'd been madly and naively in love.

When her meal arrived, she discovered that although wallowing in nostalgia hadn't made her feel the least bit inclined to weep, it had given her a ravenous appetite. She ate every last bite of the veal marsala.

After dessert she lingered over a Benedictine and observed the couples at the tables nearest her own, trying to determine which of them were dating and which were married, which were truly in love and which were simply deluding themselves. And she wondered, not for the first time, how one could tell the difference between the real thing and the short-lived emotion that turned out to be merely a cheap counterfeit.

When the waiter brought another Benedictine to her table, Darcy looked up at him in bewilderment. She hadn't ordered a second drink.

Hovering over her protectively, the waiter nodded almost imperceptibly toward a booth at the farthest corner of the room and whispered, "Compliments of the gentleman at table twenty-three."

Following the direction of the waiter's gaze, Darcy studied the man who was the lone occupant of the table.

The room was dimly lighted and the man was seated in the deepest shadows of the booth, so she couldn't make out his coloring or features. But she could tell that he was tall and ruggedly built, and as he tilted his head in her direction, she had the impression of a disturbingly handsome profile. The confident set of his shoulders, broad and powerful looking beneath the fabric of his sport coat, suggested a well-proportioned physique. If the rest of his body matched his shoulders, he must be muscular in a lean, athletic way.

She felt the intensity of his scrutiny and was torn by indecision, yet when he raised his glass to her and smiled, she yielded to impulse and signaled her acceptance of his offering by returning his salute with her own liqueur glass. Then, before she could lose her nerve, she instructed the waiter, "Tell the gentleman the lady says thank you, Giancarlo."

"*Sí*, Signora Cummins." The waiter placed her empty cordial glass on his tray. "Will there be anything else this evening?"

"Thank you, no, Giancarlo," said Darcy. "The food was as delightful as ever, but if you'll bring my check, I'll be leaving soon."

"*Sí, signora*." The waiter nodded and walked away from the table, and Darcy was left alone with her misgivings. But only momentarily.

She sensed the stranger's approach before he spoke. He was even taller and more commanding than she'd thought. He seemed to tower over her as he headed toward her table, and Darcy's qualms intensified. She glanced up at his face but had only a fleeting impression of fair hair and a square-cut jaw before she lowered her gaze. The determination she had seen in that craggy jaw intimidated her, and she dared not meet his eyes.

It was rapidly becoming evident that it would be much more difficult to control this situation than she'd thought. It was evident that the man had excellent—and expensive—taste. His necktie was patterned with a geometric design in a cream color that matched his shirt, and both shirt and tie were perfect complements to his camel-colored blazer and dark brown slacks. The quarter-inch of shirt cuff showing below the sleeves of his blazer was the exact amount dictated by fashion, and the cuffs were fastened with heavy gold cuff links.

Surreptitiously, Darcy glanced at the stranger's left hand. She half expected to find that he was wearing a wedding ring, but he wasn't. Aside from the cuff links, he wore no other jewelry; not even a wristwatch.

Though Santino's was no singles' bar, Darcy assumed he was on the make. Why else would he dress so carefully for dinner alone? Why else had he sent the drink to her table? It occurred to her that her own motives for accepting the drink were suspect, but she had no time to define them, because in that moment the stranger arrived at her table.

"May I join you?" he inquired. His voice was a reassuring baritone, carrying just the right shade of deferential courtesy, and she did not object when he took her agreement for granted and pulled out the chair opposite her own. As he seated himself, he said easily, "I saw you come in, and I thought you looked as if you'd welcome some company."

Was it a line or not, Darcy wondered. If it was, at least he'd shown some subtlety, instead of feeding her the usual cliché to the effect that lovely ladies should never dine alone. Darcy knew that she inspired a certain protectiveness in men—she supposed it was primarily due to her spectacular silver-gilt hair, which inevitably brought to mind the Hollywood stereotype of the dumb blonde. She tried to counter that image by wearing her hair in a neat chignon, eschewing makeup, and favoring chic yet tailored clothing, like the pale blue linen suit she was wearing tonight. But Darcy knew that the tailored lines of the outfit did not camouflage the womanly curves of her softly rounded figure, and she sensed that the stranger was regarding her appreciatively as he waited for her to respond to his remark.

"Is it that obvious?" she asked lightly.

She was proud of her quick response until the man reached out and touched her hand. At the brush of his fingertips against her skin, she felt a tingle of excitement, intense and unmistakable. Feigning casualness, she withdrew her hand slowly, then picked up her liqueur glass and hastily set it down again.

Had he seen the way her hand was trembling?

She toyed with the saltshaker, with some wax that

had fallen from the candle, and only then did it dawn on her that she was fidgeting, that she had been fidgeting all evening.

"I guess it is that obvious," she said, laughing self-consciously because she had answered her own question.

"Not really," said the man. "It's just that I couldn't help noticing the way you were looking at some of the couples at other tables."

For a moment she was silent. Then curiosity got the better of her and she asked, "How *did* I look at them?"

"That depended on the couple. With most of them you appeared to be mildly interested, that's all. But with one or two you seemed—well, frankly, you seemed wistful."

"You're very perceptive." Shaken by his observation, Darcy took a sip of Benedictine. She stared into the remnant of aromatic liqueur in the glass, waiting until she felt steadier to ask, "What else have you learned about me?"

"Well, for openers I've learned that you're a regular customer here, and from the way the maître d' greeted you, I'd say that you're a generous tipper." The stranger paused, and when Darcy made no response, he asked, "Shall I go on?"

"Please do," she replied evenly. "So far you're batting a thousand."

"All right then," he said, taking up the gauntlet. "Since we've established that you're a regular at Santino's, you must be fond of Italian food—"

"That's a safe assumption!"

"...and you also have a remarkably hearty appetite. Tell me, do you usually eat as much as you did tonight?"

"Only when I'm nervous."

"What are you nervous about?"

"Coming here," she replied truthfully. "I know it's silly, but it's been a long time since I've been to a restaurant like this one on my own."

"I knew that about you, too," said the man. "You've

recently been through a divorce, haven't you?"

Darcy shifted uncomfortably in her chair. This was uncanny! Could he really have intuited that she was newly divorced, or was it simply an inspired guess?

"Why do you say that?" she asked.

"Am I right?" he persisted.

"Yes," she answered tensely. "But how could you tell?"

He shrugged suggestively. "Let's just say that you have a very expressive face."

"I know," she admitted, breathing a bit easier. "There are those who accuse me of being a frustrated actress."

"And are you?"

"I suppose I am."

As she answered, without consciously planning to do so, Darcy leaned over and blew out the candle that lighted their table.

"Why did you do that?" the man asked softly.

"So I won't have to worry that you're reading everything I'm thinking in my face."

She relaxed in her chair and drank the last of the Benedictine. Now that it was dark, she felt less conspicuous, safer somehow, and she thought the stranger would be less likely to detect the way she avoided looking at him. But because she wanted to know if he'd believed her excuse, she risked a covert glance at his face.

The intimacy she saw in his smile shattered her complacency. It was so alarming that she quickly looked away again, her heart racing until she was giddy from the violent rush of adrenaline.

"Watch out," an inner voice warned. "Don't let this situation get out of control."

But over the next ten or fifteen minutes, beneath the influence of the stranger's easy banter, the worst of her fears evaporated. Not only was he surprisingly pleasant to talk with, but he was also tactful. If he noticed that she steered the conversation away from personal matters, he didn't comment on her reticence. But despite his discretion, she felt uneasy about leaving the restaurant with him. He'd placed his hand on her elbow and guided her to the door so authoritatively that she'd found herself unable to protest.

He was still holding her elbow as they crossed the parking lot. His hand was warm and strong, and he held her arm so lightly that his touch wasn't threatening in any way.

Although he shortened his stride, Darcy had to hurry to keep up with him. He moved with a coordinated grace that suggested tightly leashed power, and his step was soft for such a big man—easy, silent, and dangerous.

He walks like an Indian, she thought, or like some huge jungle cat.

Neither of them spoke until they arrived at his car. Then the stranger smiled down at her and said, "Well, Goldilocks, here we are, alone at last."

"Y–yes, so we are." Darcy looked around the parking lot frantically, wondering what he would do if she suddenly turned and fled.

As if he'd divined her thoughts, he said, "It's not too late to back out, you know."

"It's not that I want to back out," she heard herself murmur. "It's just that I'm not in the habit of doing this."

"Of course you're not," the man countered smoothly, but the cynicism in his voice made it obvious that he didn't believe her.

Feeling oddly compelled to convince him that she really wasn't accustomed to permitting strange men to pick her up, she stammered, "H–how am I doing so far?"

She was surprised when the stranger chuckled. "You're doing very well," he said. "Fact is, you're doing so well I'd never have guessed you're a novice." He paused briefly. "How am *I* doing?"

"Surely you're not a beginner, too!"

"I'm afraid so," he replied. "Oh, I might have done this once or twice before, but I'm no Don Juan."

"Well you could have fooled me."

"That's a relief," said the man, and he sounded so grateful that now it was Darcy who laughed.

His disarming frankness was all the encouragement she needed. She climbed into his car resolutely when he opened the door for her, carefully keeping her eyes downcast when the overhead light flashed on. He got in on the driver's side and, slipping his arm around her shoulders, gently drew her close.

"You're very lovely, Goldilocks," he murmured. His breath tickled her ear and sent shivers of mingled delight and trepidation up her spine. "You're the berries."

"The what?" she asked, the obscure phrase distracting her from the way his fingers lightly caressed her neck.

He chuckled low in his throat. "That just popped out. It's something we used to say in high school. If a girl was special, we called her the wood, and if she was *really* special, we called her the berries."

Darcy found herself echoing his chuckle as she tried out the phrase. "The berries? The berries..."

She liked his spontaneity, his candor. Without willing it, she nestled her head against his neck, and suddenly something inside her that had been closed for a long time opened. The last of her inner reserve melted away and she let down her guard in a way she hadn't since the early days of Tim's courtship.

When the stranger brushed his lips against her ear, it seemed the most natural thing in the world. As if he sensed her receptivity, he pulled her closer to him, enfolding her in an all-encompassing embrace, and she went into his arms willingly, relaxing against his broad, muscular chest, wrapping her own arms around his neck and clinging to him, melting into the hard angles of his body. And when he kissed her, the last of her fears were dispelled.

There was no game-playing, no deceit, in the way his mouth moved over hers, in the way he teased her lips apart with the tip of his tongue. There was only the hot, open-mouthed hunger of a man for a woman. His hands were honest, too. They were gentle and sure as they caressed her back, molding her closer to him. They were knowing and persuasive as they learned the satiny texture of her skin.

For a time Darcy gave herself over to the sensations he was evoking. Wildly excited by the way his hair curled so crisply around her fingers, by his clean male scent, by the intoxicating brandy taste of his tongue and the silken glide of his hands as he caressed her, she responded to his overtures as she never had been able to before, eagerly returning kiss for kiss and touch for touch.

But in the end it was the stranger's very lack of pretense that caused her to put an end to their lovemaking.

"My place or yours?" he whispered.

"Wha—what?" Sanity returned, and Darcy realized that she couldn't handle the situation after all.

"Shall we go to my place or yours?" he repeated.

Wedging her arms between them, she flattened her hands against his chest and pushed with more force than was actually necessary; for at the first sign of her resistance, he released her.

Sagging weakly against the passenger door, Darcy ducked her head so that a strand of hair that had escaped from her chignon slipped forward to veil her face. She couldn't make herself look at the stranger.

"I'm sorry," she apologized lamely. "It seems I can't go through with this."

"That much is apparent," he said coolly. "But if you really don't usually go in for this sort of thing, why the hell did you have to make an exception with me?"

"Maybe it's because I received my final divorce papers today—"

"And you wanted to prove to yourself that you're still desirable?" he offered sardonically.

"N—no, not that! It was more that I wanted to prove I could still *feel* something."

"That's rich!" Out of the corner of her eye, Darcy saw that the man's hands were knotted into fists with the effort of controlling his temper. "Don't try to tell me you didn't feel anything when I was kissing you just now, because I could tell you *did*."

"I'm not denying that." How could she deny it when this stranger had awakened a depth of passion in her that she'd never experienced with Tim? "I'm not sure I can explain it so you'll understand," she said miserably. "I'm not even sure I understand it myself, but it wasn't long ago that I loved my ex-husband so much I would have agreed to almost any terms if only he would come back to me. Then, for a while, I was furious because he didn't come back, and after that I was terribly bitter because all our separation seemed to mean to him was that I might insist on keeping our season tickets to the Huskies' games. And now that our marriage is officially over, it didn't seem right that I felt *nothing*. I mean, even if it were still painful, that would be better than nothing, wouldn't it? But I'm not grief-stricken or angry. I'm not even bitter anymore. Then you sent the drink to my table, and I thought—"

"You thought I might do as a stand-in for your ex-husband," the stranger suggested angrily. "You've been pretending I'm him, and that's why you haven't looked at me."

Darcy sighed unhappily. "Something like that. I guess I was looking for some kind of catharsis . . ." She let her voice trail off, unable to explain even to herself.

"You thought," he said more calmly, "that maybe I'd help you revive some of those old feelings."

"I suppose I did think that," she reluctantly admitted.

"What stopped you, then?"

"You did."

"I did?" His laugh was tinged with irony and incredulity. "Please, go on. This is getting better and better."

"Well, you made no secret of the fact that you wanted me—"

"Are you saying you didn't want me?" he demanded.

"No," she whispered. "What I'm saying is that I wanted

something very different than a brief sexual encounter, and I suddenly felt like a fraud. You were honest with me, and I was repaying you by being dishonest and selfish—and cheap—"

"I get the picture, Goldilocks." The edge had gone out of his voice now. "Listen," he relented, "you're blaming yourself a whole lot more than you should. You made a mistake, but it's all over now and no damage was done. Would you like me to drive you home?"

"No! That is, I have my own car."

"Shall I walk you to your car, then?"

"I appreciate the offer, but I'd really rather you didn't."

"Sure," he said quietly. "I understand."

He reached over to open her door, and she stepped out of the car quickly. She still avoided looking at him. After the wanton way she'd behaved, she wished only to escape.

It was not until she was driving homeward through the soft summer night that Darcy realized how anonymous the whole encounter had been. She doubted that she'd recognize the stranger if they ever chanced to meet again—it had been so dark in the restaurant, and even darker in the car. It was as if the fates had conspired with her in her effort to recapture some of the tenderness she'd once felt for Tim.

What's more, she didn't know the man's name—nor did he know hers. She was appalled by what she had almost done, by the passion with which she'd responded to his advances. But her own anonymity was comforting.

Because of her parents' renown, anonymity—or, as Darcy's mother termed it, obscurity—was a relatively new luxury to Darcy. She prized it enormously and guarded it jealously. Her maiden name was so prominent, she'd decided to continue using her married name despite the divorce.

Years ago the Lunts had electrified theater audiences. Later it was Hepburn and Tracy, and still later movie-goers thrilled to the performances of Ariel and Darryl

St. Denis. Their appeal had not diminished, in spite of her father's death and her mother's retirement, and in the last decade, thanks to television late shows, a whole new generation of fans had been captivated by her parents' artistry.

As she drove across Lake Washington on the Mercer Island Floating Bridge, Darcy acknowledged that Tim's surname provided her with a welcome buffer, preventing the bothersome instant recognition that she was the daughter of the legendary St. Denises. After she'd married Tim, for the first time in her life she had begun to feel like a person in her own right.

Of course, Darcy cautioned herself, it was possible that Tim himself would become famous someday. With his suave good looks and boyish smile, he certainly fulfilled the requirements for a matinee idol, and after the convincing role he'd played for her—appearing contented with a partnership in his father's insurance agency when all the while he was scheming to trade on her connections to launch a career in films—perhaps Tim had the talent to succeed as an actor as well.

But if Tim planned to make it to the top of the heap by using the same cutthroat tactics he'd started out with, she doubted he had the grit to survive in the movie industry.

Darcy had to admit that Tim had used *her* readily enough, but since she'd been thrown completely off-balance by the excitement of her first love affair, she had been a comparatively easy mark.

Once he'd gained entree to her parents' world, however, it hadn't taken him long to look for the next rung up the ladder. Before their first anniversary Tim had confessed that he was having an affair with Nina Ludlow, whose father was a producer at one of the major studios. And Nina, Darcy knew, played ball in an entirely different league, making up the rules to suit herself as she went along.

If the rumors Darcy had heard lately about the widening rift between Tim and Nina were true, Tim was already taking more than his share of lumps. He might make it to the top or he might not, but in any case, Darcy would not have to cope with any reflected glory of Tim's.

Even if he achieved the superstardom he coveted, Cummins was a much less distinctive name than St. Denis. Besides, their marriage had been so brief and, much to Tim's dismay, so unpublicized, that no one except personal acquaintances would ever make the connection between Darcy and her ex-husband.

In the nearly two years since she and Tim had separated, Darcy had adopted a philosophical attitude toward their breakup. As she often told herself, it could have been much worse. At least, when the end came, Tim had paid her the courtesy of being candid. He'd told her quite bluntly that he believed Nina would be more help to him in achieving his ambitions than she could ever hope to be.

There was no arguing with that, Darcy thought firmly, and she hadn't felt capable of competing with Nina's sultry beauty either. But by now, if the truth were told, even if she could have competed with Nina Ludlow, she wouldn't have wanted to. If Tim looked upon a wife as a mere stepping-stone to fame, she didn't want to be the one he stepped on.

In all honesty, now that she had made a complete fool of herself with the stranger, now that she had paid a final tribute to Tim by poking and prodding her psyche and playing out the charade at Santino's, she had to admit that she was vastly relieved to have gotten out of her marriage so lightly.

Perhaps this was why, when her mother phoned the next evening, Darcy's conscience was sending out vague twinges of guilt, as if it were she rather than Tim who had betrayed their wedding vows.

"Honestly, darling!" Ariel exclaimed when Darcy had

given her an expurgated account of how she'd spent the previous night. "I can't believe you actually went through with it."

"I don't know why not," Darcy replied defensively. "When we talked yesterday, I told you what my plans were."

"True, but I thought you might have the good sense to change your mind. I mean, what was the point of your having dinner at Santino's, of all places?"

At the moment Darcy didn't feel capable of answering this question, and when she didn't reply, Ariel crowed, "I always knew you should have become an actress! You have more talent for overdramatizing a situation than any ten other people. If that's not exactly like you, .going through that whole sentimental rigamarole to commemorate a marriage that never should have happened to begin with!"

"Well, Mother," Darcy returned equably, "if I do tend to overdramatize things, it's a talent I've come by naturally."

"Touché, darling," Ariel retorted laughing. "But I'd like you to answer one question—if you can. Why shouldn't you be relieved to have the debacle with Tim behind you?"

"I'm not sure, Mother," Darcy replied hesitantly.

"You haven't even *seen* Tim Cummins for eighteen months," Ariel returned astringently. "And you cried the proverbial river when he first walked out on you. I could understand that because, to give the devil his due, Tim's a charmer. But the time for tears is past, love. Now is the time for rejoicing. Now that you've finally been liberated from your mésalliance to one of the greatest world-class rat-finks of all time, you should be celebrating!"

Darcy couldn't help laughing at Ariel's outspokenness as she asked, "And how would you suggest I celebrate?"

"By finding yourself a new man, of course. Is there any other way?"

If only her mother knew how perilously close she had

come to following that recommendation! Choking back a groan, Darcy cried, "I should have known you'd say that!"

"Naturally you should," Ariel blithely allowed. "After all, I've been open about my own love affairs, and you know I've always contended that the best antidote for an unhappy love affair is to start another one—the sooner the better! You have to use it or lose it, darling."

Through gritted teeth, Darcy said, "All *right*, Mother. But even if I were to concede that my happiness and well-being were dependent upon my having a man in my bed, I'm not ready for a casual affair."

With an expressive little ripple of laughter, Ariel inquired, "Who said anything about casual?"

"Mother!" In spite of her attempt to remain calm, Darcy's protest was shrill. "You never give up, do you? Right now there's only one thing that has less appeal than a casual fling, and that's a serious involvement."

For a few moments Ariel was silent, and when she finally spoke, a note of conciliation had crept into her voice.

"Since you've ruled out my number-one prescription, may I propose an alternative?"

"I sincerely wish you would," Darcy answered.

"I'm coming up to Roche Harbor this weekend. Why don't you come with me?"

"There's nothing I'd like more, Mother, but I'm scheduled to work Saturday morning."

"Surely the library can survive with a substitute story lady for *one* day. Exchange your hours with someone else, Darcy. You've always loved the island, and it's been ages since you've been there."

"You're right about that. As a matter of fact, I didn't even know you'd opened up the cabin."

"I haven't," Ariel admitted. "Not for several years. It's just not worth the hassle for the little time I spend there, and by myself I positively rattle around in that big old house."

"Where will you stay, then? At the De Haro?"

"No, not at the hotel. I've been invited to stay with Jennifer Lazenby. You remember Jenny, don't you?"

"Just barely. I saw her in passing maybe half a dozen times when we were at Roche Harbor the summer after Daddy died, and I've heard you speak of her."

"Well, let me assure you that 'the more, the merrier' is Jenny's motto. She'd *adore* to have you join the party!"

"Party?" Darcy echoed faintly. "What kind of party?"

"Didn't I mention it, darling?" said Ariel, laughing gaily. "I must be getting absent-minded in my old age. Jenny's invited a few other people, but she hadn't planned anything elaborate. It's going to be a nice, typically quiet San Juan Island weekend."

Darcy was skeptical. Ariel St. Denis might be fifty-seven, but she looked at least fifteen years younger, and she abhorred peace and quiet.

"Tell you what, Mother," Darcy said crisply. "Why don't you cancel your arrangements to go to Roche Harbor and spend a few days here in Seattle instead? I could take some of the vacation time I've got coming, and we might even go over to Victoria together."

"No." Ariel's reply was succinct to the point of sounding testy, but she softened it by explaining, "I simply cannot go back on my word to Jen, Darcy. She has enough on her mind just now without having her oldest and dearest friend desert her."

So Jennifer Lazenby was in some predicament, thought Darcy, and Ariel, loyal friend that she was, was charging to the rescue. In light of this information, her suspicions that Jenny's houseguests included a man that Ariel saw as a likely successor to Tim Cummins were allayed.

"I'm frightfully worried about Jenny," Ariel disclosed without prompting. "I'm afraid she's seriously contemplating getting married again."

"Now, that's priceless," Darcy teased. "After the way you've promoted romance as a panacea for everything from hangnails to ulcers, I should think the idea of Jenny getting married would make you want to stand up and cheer."

"If it were anyone except Jen Lazenby, that's precisely what I'd do, but Jenny has the most wretched taste in men, Darcy! She's been married four times, and each of her husbands has left her quite a lot poorer and not a whit wiser. And from the little I've seen of her latest, he's nothing but a gigolo who'll really take her to the cleaners if someone doesn't put a stop to her foolishness."

"Mother," Darcy said gently, "I admire you for wanting to help your friend, but when are you going to learn that people don't appreciate that kind of interference in their lives?"

"But she's asked for my opinion!"

"That doesn't mean she's prepared to listen to it."

"Whether she listens or not, I intend to talk some sense into her," Ariel declared emphatically. "And now that that's settled, can I count on seeing my darling daughter this weekend, or must I continue to worry about you via long distance?"

Darcy got no further than, "Really, Mother, I don't think—" when Ariel interrupted.

"Look, dear," she said with just the slightest trace of petulance, "I know you haven't even begun to give me all the reasons why you can't come with me to Roche Harbor, but in the end you're going to agree to it. You know you are, just as you know I have your best interests at heart in asking. And since my phone bill is going to read like the national debt if I have to listen to all of your arguments, why don't you simply say you'll meet me in Anacortes at noon on Friday?"

With a sigh of resignation Darcy said, "If I'm taking Saturday off, I can't possibly get away from the library before Friday afternoon."

"Then I'll expect you to be on the ferry that evening. See you then, darling."

Before Darcy could reply, Ariel had broken the connection. But that was typical. When, Darcy reminded herself, had she *ever* won an argument with her mother? For that matter, when had *anyone?*

When she was a little girl, it had seemed to Darcy that her mother was infinitely wise, and to this day, whatever Ariel coaxed, wheedled, or verbally bludgeoned her into doing usually *did* turn out to be for her own good. But that, Darcy acknowledged, only made Ariel's advice the more maddening.

As she showered and prepared for bed, Darcy felt oddly lighthearted. The idea of spending the weekend at Roche Harbor became more appealing by the minute, and it was not until much later, when she was lying in her darkened bedroom on the brink of sleep, that it occurred to her that Ariel had not given her the smallest clue as to who Jenny Lazenby's other houseguests were going to be.

Chapter 2

THE GEMLIKE ISLANDS that made up the San Juan Ar-
chipelago were scattered in an uneven crescent between
the Washington state mainland and Vancouver Island.
They were bounded on the south by Puget Sound and on
the north by the Strait of Georgia, while the gateway to
the Pacific, the Strait of Juan de Fuca, lay immediately
to the southwest.

The waters thereabouts were notorious for the treach-
erous chop they could develop given the right combination of wind and tide, and the Friday night crossing
to San Juan Island was a rough one. The ferry lurched
over mountainous waves, only to slide into a sickening
roll in the troughs between the swells.

Darcy, who was usually quite a good sailor, stood on
the afterdeck watching the lights of Anacortes slip away
behind the stern of the ferry, and before they had faded

out of sight, she knew her stomach must be churning as violently as the inky water of the channel.

They made routine stops at Lopez, Shaw, and Orcas Islands, and it was eleven o'clock when the ferry tied up to the dock at Friday Harbor. By then Darcy knew what prompted seamen to get down on their knees and kiss the ground of whatever port happened to be their landfall. Never had she imagined that the solid feel of dry land beneath her feet could make her so deliriously happy!

She still felt queasy, but once she was safely ashore, things began to look brighter. Her Mazda was one of the first cars the crew offloaded, and the drive to Roche Harbor was accomplished in record time. Within a matter of minutes she was parking the car near the portico of Jenny Lazenby's house.

The windows were ablaze with lights, allowing Darcy a fairly good view of the house. It was handsomely mellowed with age, and the boxy lines of its facade were softened by large bay windows, a round towerlike structure at one corner, and the ivy that trailed lushly over its cedar and fieldstone outer walls.

As she climbed out of the car and wearily collected her luggage, she caught a glimpse of the emerald velvet of well-kept lawns sweeping down to the stand of pines that guarded the shoreline.

Darcy set off purposefully down the walk, but before she had reached the broad, shallow steps, where tree roses planted in tubs marked the pathway from the forecourt to the front entry, the door was thrown wide and she was being welcomed by the housekeeper, who introduced herself as Olive Hyatt.

A pleasant-faced woman of indeterminate age, Olive took one look at Darcy and remarked, "I heard on the late news that the channel's really kicking up tonight. Shall I show you to your room, or do you feel up to joining the others in the den? You're the last to arrive—except Jordan, of course."

"If you'll make my apologies for me and tell my mother I'm here, I think I'd prefer to go straight to my room," Darcy replied.

Moments later, Olive was ushering her along the luxuriously carpeted hall that branched away from the foyer into what was evidently a bedroom wing of the house. "You'll be staying in one of the tower rooms," the housekeeper said, indicating a door near the end of the corridor. "Your mother's room is just next door. Mr. and Mrs. Perrigo are across from her—"

"Have they any connection with Perrigo Wines?"

"They *are* Perrigo Wines." Olive's lips twitched into a dry smile before she continued briskly, "They're here for some sort of pow-wow with Miles Bruckner, who handles their advertising. His room's next to theirs. Mrs. Lazenby likes the morning sun, so her room is in the family wing, along with Mr. Templeton's. When Jordan gets here, he'll have the room directly above this one."

Hoping she did not look as strained as she felt at the prospect of having to sort out the identities of all these people, Darcy smiled. Then, because Olive seemed to expect her to make some comment on the assembly, she said, "I'm looking forward to meeting the others."

Olive must have been satisfied with this pleasantry because she opened the door and showed Darcy into the tower room. Darcy was delighted to see that it faced the harbor, but she gained only a fleeting impression of its elegant appointments as she hurried toward the windows to look out at the view.

She could not actually see the moon, but it paved a shimmering silver path upon the darkly rippling surface of the water. The town of Roche Harbor seemed to be fast asleep. With the exception of the moonlight and a small cluster of lights from the Hotel De Haro, the darkness was complete. And except for an oceangoing ketch that was just rounding the point near Pearl Island, everything was still.

Initially, she could see only the faint flicker of the

running lights of the ketch. Then, as they caught the gusting wind, the sails filled, and their smooth white swell reflected the moonlight. Arrested by the serene beauty of the boat, Darcy dropped down onto the window seat and watched the ketch's progress as it glided silently toward the marina.

After checking the supply of towels in the bathroom and turning back the bedcovers, Olive came to the windows and joined Darcy in watching the sailboat.

"That'll be the *Compass Rose,*" she said.

"The *Compass Rose?*" Darcy echoed. "What a marvelous name for a sailboat! Does it have some special significance?"

"It does," Olive replied. "The way Jordan explained it to me when he named her, a compass rose is what they call the graduated compass circles that are printed on charts. It's a navigation aid that shows how to correct from magnetic north to true north. Jordan says that without the compass rose the course a sea captain charts would be off by several degrees. And let me tell you, Jordan is a great one for staying on course. Once he sets his sights on something, they stay set till he's got what he's after!"

Darcy's curiosity was aroused by this outburst. Thinking that Jordan, whoever he might be, must be frightfully intrepid, she cast a quizzical glance at Olive. Only then did she become aware that the housekeeper was patiently waiting to complete the task of acquainting her with her room.

"I hope you'll be comfortable here," said Olive.

"With this view of the water, how could I not be?" asked Darcy.

For the first time she noticed how charming the bedroom was. Its predominating colors were pastel coral and ivory, and the rich maplewood of the antique armoire and bureau shone with a warm patina of care in the lamplight. Because of the way the walls curved on two sides of the room, Darcy thought that sleeping in the graceful spindle bed would be as cozy as sleeping in a seashell.

The drawer of the nightstand contained a floor plan of the house, which would simplify the problem of finding her way about. Olive referred to it as she got on with the business of familiarizing Darcy with the amenities of the suite, but by then Darcy was paying scant attention.

The tangy salt breeze that drifted through the open windows carried with it the scent of roses and the resinous fragrance of pine. It also brought the sweetly distracting sound of music. As tantalizing snatches of a delicately baroque melody floated up to Darcy, she realized that someone in the harbor had tuned his receiver to a mainland station. Looking down at the forest of ships' masts in the marina, she listened more closely. The direction the music came from changed several times—now advancing, now retreating—which meant it must be coming from the cabin of the *Compass Rose*.

A familiar passage of counterpoint enabled Darcy to identify the piece as Pachelbel's "Canon in D," a favorite of hers.

How strange, thought Darcy. From the little Olive had told her about the owner of the *Compass Rose,* she would have expected his taste in music to run to something strident and martial—Wagner perhaps, or hard rock. She certainly wouldn't have guessed he'd enjoy the hauntingly lyrical Canon.

Just who was Jordan, she wondered, and why did Olive Hyatt's eyes shine with fondness every time she said his name?

Before Darcy could pursue this intriguing line of inquiry any further, Olive spoke.

"If you're sure you have everything you need, I'll leave you now. One of the maids will bring you some tea in half an hour or so. If you want anything in the meantime, you can buzz me on the intercom."

"That will be fine, Olive," Darcy replied. "Thanks for your time."

"Don't mention it." With a self-deprecating shrug, the housekeeper moved toward the hallway, but when she reached the open door, she paused. Turning, she smiled amiably and said, "I hope you'll have a pleasant stay with us, Darcy."

Early the next morning, as Darcy strolled toward the house her mother's father had built, it seemed that the weekend would be a very pleasant one indeed. After a leisurely bath, a good night's sleep, and a hearty breakfast of scrambled eggs and blueberry muffins washed down with two cups of Olive Hyatt's fabulous coffee, she felt revitalized.

Knowing that Ariel, who had been playing bridge into the wee hours of the morning, wouldn't stir from her room before noon, Darcy decided to take a walk. She ambled along, dangling her floppy-brimmed straw hat from one hand, drinking in the ambience of Roche Harbor as she went. She savored the warmth of the sun and the windswept blue of the sky, and admired the filigree of dew drops that sparkled in the grasses, giving even such a mundane object as a spider's web its own rare beauty.

Although Roche Harbor had originated as a company town in the 1800s, there was a timeless quality about it that Darcy supposed must be comprised of equal portions of its long tradition of resistance to change, the incredible natural beauty of the island's virgin forests and sheltered coves, and its separateness from the mainland.

Today the very air had a crystalline clarity that was as heady as wine—and every bit as intoxicating. After taking a few deep breaths of it, the workaday worries of her life in Seattle seemed remote and even foolish. There was a spring in Darcy's step that proclaimed she was ready to take on the whole world if she had to, but there was no need to hurry.

As she stooped down to remove a pebble that had worked its way into her thonged sandal, Darcy thought that if only old John Stanford McMillin had known the effect of the harbor air when he'd come to the San Juan Islands back in the 1880s, he might never have bothered with the Lime Company, which he'd established at Roche Harbor. Instead, he would have simply bottled the air and made his fortune that way.

When she straightened and looked around her, Darcy saw that she had reached the trail she'd always used as a shortcut from the town to her mother's house. Her steps quickened with anticipation as she left the street to plunge through the narrow gap in the underbrush.

The trail wound uphill through a grove of hemlock and fir. In her eagerness to see the house Darcy was running when she reached the top of the hill and began the descent on the other side. But her feet dragged to a stop when she came out of the trees and arrived at a clearing where she had an unrestricted view of the rambling Dutch Colonial dwelling.

Her eyes widened with surprise when she saw the condition of the house. It was not at all as she remembered it. In the old days, when her father was alive and her parents had come here regularly, it had been painted a fresh, spanking white. The trim and shutters had been a sharp black that showed off the old-rose tones of the brick facing.

Now there was an air of sad indigence about the house. Like an aging beauty, its paint was chalking and flaking. There were patches where the paint had peeled away to the bare wood of the siding. Most of the shutters were missing, and those that remained were broken.

From her vantage point on the side of the hill, Darcy could see that the acre of lawn which surrounded the house was weedy and badly needed mowing. But as she moved closer to the house, she noticed that the climbing roses still rioted on the trellises along the breezeway to the garage.

Unlike the house, the roses were thriving despite neglect. They grew in a defiant profusion of color, creating vibrant splashes of red, yellow, and pink against the weathered gray of the breezeway wall, perfuming the air and tempting passing swarms of fat, lazy bumblebees to sample their nectar.

Why had her mother allowed the place to become so run-down, Darcy wondered with some dismay. Not only was this Ariel's childhood home, but Ariel's father had built it, and Ariel had always looked upon it as a shrine to his memory. She'd told Darcy that she and Darryl had spent some of their happiest times here.

Puzzled, Darcy reached out and plucked one of the roses, then another and another. She had picked a dozen or more blooms when a deep masculine voice said, "Help yourself."

Darcy started and scratched herself on a thorn. The voice had come from somewhere above and slightly behind her. Dropping the roses, she spun around and looked toward the roof of the garage.

The first thing her disbelieving eyes encountered was a pair of sneaker-clad feet. Her gaze slanted upward, following long, powerful legs that seemed to go on forever, skidding past narrow hips and a flat belly only to linger admiringly on the well-defined muscles of a broad masculine chest.

The sun was directly behind the man and she had to shade her eyes with one hand in order to see his face. As her eyes adjusted to the glare, she could see his thatch of crisply curling light-brown hair, and when she met his eyes, she saw that they were a startling electric blue and were boldly returning her appraisal.

Against her will, her own hazel eyes trailed downward once more, taking in the man's naked chest and the tawny cloud of hair that tapered down to the belt of the faded cutoff jeans riding low on his lean hips.

He was wearing only the cutoffs and the sneakers, and he hadn't even bothered to tie his shoelaces. Before she could stop herself, Darcy found herself wondering if the parts of him that weren't exposed were as magnificent as the parts that were.

It required a supreme exertion of will to tear her bemused gaze away from his body. When she glanced at
his face again, she saw the faintly mocking awareness
with which he was watching her and she *knew* that he'd
read her thoughts.

All at once the sun that beat down on her upturned
face seemed unbearably hot, so hot that she felt flushed
and overheated.

"P-pardon me," she stammered. "What was it you
said?"

"I said help yourself," the man replied.

"To what?" asked Darcy, thoroughly flustered. Surely
he couldn't be telling her to help herself to *him!*

"Why, to the roses, of course. What else?" said the
man.

His suggestive tone of voice and playful expression
told her in no uncertain terms that he'd invaded her mind
and ferreted out her thoughts yet again. That his husky
drawl was so familiar added to her confusion. Her blush
deepened until her face felt as if it were on fire, but the
simple expedient of putting on her sun hat to conceal her
embarrassment occurred to her only after the man had
seen the first revealing rush of color to her cheeks.

Even so, she jammed the hat on her head, hastily
tucked her hair beneath the fragile shield the lacy weave
of the straw provided, pulled at the brim so that it dipped
even lower over her face, and finally knotted the scarf
that secured the hat, tying it tightly under her chin. But
all her frantic activity only caused the man to throw his
head back and laugh outright at her discomfiture.

Although her own face was now as deeply shad-
owed as his, she still felt at a distinct disadvantage.
Perhaps it had something to do with the way he stood
there at the edge of the roof, looking down at her as if
he were an incarnation of Apollo standing on the summit
of Olympus. Much as she wanted to, she couldn't seem
to stop staring back at him.

There was something about him—something in the

bright flash of his smile, something in the way he tilted his head—that was terribly familiar. And his voice— she was *certain* now that she'd heard it somewhere before. But where? If they had ever been introduced, she would have remembered him.

Blast him! thought Darcy. It was bad enough that he was insufferably rude and impossibly arrogant. Why, oh why, did he have to be so damned handsome! It was indecent, really, that he should look like the exact composite of all the lovers she had ever fantasized about.

Not that she'd ever done anything about her fantasies. She'd had only one lover, and she'd been married to him. And as it had turned out, she'd never completely lost her inhibitions with Tim. She wasn't sure why, but when she was with him, she'd always felt too self-conscious to let herself go. Whatever the reason, while her experience with him hadn't been a rude awakening, neither had it been a dream.

When they'd separated, Ariel had told her, "It's not enough to dream, Darcy. The trouble with you is that you're not willing to take the necessary action to make your dreams come true. You've got to wake up and start *living*."

Well, perhaps Ariel was right. Maybe she had allowed herself to settle into a comfortable, well-worn rut. Maybe that was why she'd felt so dissatisfied lately. And if it was time to wake up and start living, was there a better way to begin than by trying to pique the interest of this man—this perfect stranger?

The problem was, she hadn't the foggiest idea how to go about it, and at the moment she felt more exasperated than romantic. How could she feel like a sensuous woman when she was wearing the denim shorts and sun halter she'd had since high school and her hair was straggling out of its chignon?

And to top it all off, she was getting sunburned! From the way the skin across her shoulders and at the backs of her knees was starting to sting, she knew if she didn't get out of the sun soon, she'd have to spend the rest of the weekend recuperating. Besides, the way the stranger was watching her was making her feel more uncomfortable with every passing second.

"If you don't mind," she said crossly, "I'd appreciate your telling me what you're doing up there."

"Oh, but I do mind," he replied easily. "I've made it a hard and fast rule never to play cards with a guy named Doc, never to eat at a place called Mom's, and I never answer leading questions unless I know who's asking them."

"Touché!" she called back, falling into the spirit of his repartee. "Since my credentials seem to be in question, I suppose I should tell you that my mother owns this house."

"Then you must be Darcy St. Denis."

"Darcy Cummins," she corrected him coolly, wondering how he'd learned her first name. "Do you know my mother?" she asked.

"Sure. I've known Ariel for years."

Going down on one knee, the man found a handhold on the gutter, tested it to see if it would support his weight, and swung down from the roof, landing lithely on the balls of his feet at Darcy's side. "Ariel's the one who asked me to take a look at the roof and see what it'll take to repair it," he explained.

So he was a roofing contractor, thought Darcy, pleased that she had an answer to at least one of her questions. Aloud, she inquired, "What *will* it take?"

"There are about six different layers of roofing material up there already," he replied, studying the house with a critical eye, "so I'm afraid it's going to be a major project. All the old shakes will have to come off before a new roof can go on, which means, of course, that you'll have to be concerned about weight distribution on the bearing walls."

"Of course," Darcy agreed when he trailed into silence. "But what I can't help wondering is why my mother let the house get into such a state in the first place."

"Maybe she didn't have the wherewithal to maintain it." Shrugging, the man turned away from the house to glance at Darcy. "You knew she's going to put the house on the market, didn't you?"

"No, I didn't. She never said a thing about selling to me. Are you sure—"

"Yes, I am. That's why she's so anxious to get it fixed up."

"Do you know when she wants to list it?"

"She didn't say, but I got the impression she'd like to have it off her hands before the end of the summer."

Completely mystified, Darcy asked, "Are you a realtor, then?"

"Nope."

Although she waited for him to expand on his reply, a single emphatic shake of his head was all he added. Had she been right the first time, she wondered. Was he a contractor after all?

Her eyes were wide and troubled as she looked up at him. Now that he was standing so close to her, the raw animal magnetism he exuded was incredibly potent. She felt a sudden need to touch him, to reassure herself that he was flesh and blood and not a figment of her imagination.

Equally imperative, however, was the need to fight this compulsion. But when she knelt to pick up the roses she'd dropped, he sat on his heels and helped her gather them. When they had finished, he handed her the roses he'd collected, and still avoiding his gaze, Darcy buried her face in the silky coolness of the blossoms.

"They're already starting to wilt," she observed sadly.

"So are you, Goldilocks," he said softly. "You're getting sunburned."

Goldilocks! Dear heaven! No wonder his voice had sounded familiar.

"It's *you!*" she gasped, staring at him in bewildered disbelief. "But it can't be! You—you're the man from—from—"

"Santino's," he acknowledged. "We meet again, Goldilocks. I must say, it took you long enough to recognize me."

"B-but the other night you were wearing—" She saw the laughter in his eyes, blushed hotly, and tried again. "It was dark and—er, I was upset."

"So I gathered."

"Oh, Lord! This is so embarrassing!"

"Why? There's not much virtue without temptation. Both of us made a mistake that night, but if that's the worst thing either of us has ever done, we're basically pretty decent people."

In spite of this reassurance Darcy wished she could disappear. She wanted to run away, to escape his penetrating gaze, but she couldn't seem to move a muscle. She was riveted by the intense blue of his eyes as he removed one of the flowers from her bouquet and touched the rose to her cheek, to the delicate line of her jaw. He brushed the rose along her mouth, and finally over the bare skin of her shoulder. Then, holding his forearm close to hers, he compared his own burnished tan with her indoor pallor.

"You really are the fairest of them all," he marveled. "It's obvious you don't get outdoors anywhere near often enough."

"N-not as much as I'd like to."

Despite the warmth of the sun and the heat that radiated from his body, she shivered. Jumping to her feet, she announced in a stilted voice, "I should be going now."

The man rose more slowly, studying her intently all the while. "What's your hurry?" he asked.

"Well, as you pointed out, the sun's beginning to get to me—"

"Where are you staying?" he cut in.

"At Jenny Lazenby's."

He nodded before she'd gotten the words out. It was almost as if he'd anticipated her answer.

"Then you'll need something to cover up with for the walk back." With that, he strode away from her, saying, "I left my shirt around here somewhere."

He moved out of sight, beyond the corner of the garage, and when he reappeared a few seconds later, he was carrying a madras plaid sport shirt.

"Put this on," he said, holding the shirt out to her.

When Darcy only stared at the garment, surprised by the chivalrous gesture, he draped the shirt around her shoulders himself. She slipped her arms into the sleeves automatically, but while he was buttoning it, she found her voice and uttered a belated protest.

"I can't take your shirt!"

"Why not?" he demanded. "You need it more than I do just now. You'll be burned to a crisp without it."

"But I'm going back to Seattle tomorrow evening. How will I return it to you?"

"Never fear, Goldilocks." He lifted the brim of her hat, dropped a kiss on the tip of her nose, and smiled at her astonished expression. Leaning close to her, he whispered, "I have no intention of losing my—uh, shirt. I'll know where to find it when I want it."

Darcy was speechless. The innuendo was unmistakable—he was implying that she was his for the taking and that when he wanted her, he would claim her.

She was stunned and outraged and more than a little excited by his presumption, but before she could formulate a reply, he had moved away from her and was walking along the breezeway, stopping now and again to examine a window sash or dig at the fascia under the eaves with the pocketknife he had fished out of the hip pocket of his cutoffs.

Thinking that in many ways he was the most extraordinary man she had ever met, she cried, "What in the world are you doing now?"

"Checking for dry rot," he replied absently, already deeply absorbed in the job at hand.

Fascinated by the lightning-fast refocusing of his attention, Darcy watched after him until he had reached the end of the breezeway. He had opened the side door of the house and was stepping across the threshold before she thought to call out, "Wait a minute—I don't even know your name!"

The man raised one hand, waving a jaunty farewell. "It's Jordan," he called. "Jordan Ives."

Chapter 3

So MUCH FOR flights of fancy, Darcy told herself wryly as she began the long trek back to the Lazenby house.

Once again she had been victimized by her overactive imagination. When Jordan Ives had said he had no intention of losing his shirt, she had taken a simple hesitation of speech, magnified it out of any reasonable proportion, and made a quantum leap to the conclusion that he was actually saying he did not intend to lose *her*. But now that she knew his identity, it was painfully obvious that she'd been mistaken. Jordan had merely been enjoying his own private joke. Since they were both staying at Jenny's, naturally he wasn't at all concerned about recovering his property.

Had her foolish assumption been apparent to Jordan, she wondered. Had he been laughing at her?

Darcy had no way of knowing, but if she hadn't felt so chagrined, she might have laughed at herself. Heaven

knew that anyone who could reach the age of twenty-
seven and still be so pathetically susceptible to romantic
illusion *deserved* to be laughed at.

Nevertheless, when she stopped in at the old Roche
Harbor cemetery to lay the roses she'd picked on her
grandfather's grave, she couldn't make herself leave the
rose Jordan had used to caress her face with the rest of
the bouquet. As she was latching the gate to her grandfather's gravesite behind herself, it occurred to her that
she really ought to have some small souvenir from the
house Grandfather Massie had built, and if Ariel sold
the place, she probably wouldn't have another chance to
collect one.

This was all very logical, but it didn't begin to explain
why she sifted through the flowers and finally selected
that particular rose.

Two hours later, Darcy was standing in front of the
armoire in the tower room trying to decide what to wear
for lunch, which Olive Hyatt had told her was to be
served on the terrace.

Darcy's forehead was creased with perplexity as she
surveyed the clothes she'd brought for the weekend. For
some reason, she was dissatisfied with every garment in
her wardrobe, but out of necessity she settled on a cream-
colored muslin peasant dress as being the best of a sorry
lot.

Sighing, she wandered to the bureau, found some
fresh underwear in the top drawer, and quickly, before
she could change her mind again, slipped out of her
cotton kimono.

Within seconds she had stepped into the panties and
pulled on the camisole and the dress. As she tied the
drawstring at the bodice of the dress and adjusted the
drape of the skirt about her slender hips, she gave herself
a much needed pep talk.

"Where do you think you're going—to a ball?" she

demanded of her reflection in the mirror. "What are you trying to prove? More to the point, *who* are you trying to prove it to? This is only a simple lunch, but you're acting as if it were a banquet at the Taj Mahal!"

That was true enough. Her image offered tangible proof of the unconscionable amount of time she had devoted to her appearance.

After a long, deliciously cool shower, lavish applications of a sinfully expensive moisturizer, and a light dusting with talcum, her sunburn was barely noticeable. Only the faintest hint of color could be seen on her forearms and the tops of her shoulders—just enough to give her skin the creamy translucence of a pink pearl.

She had washed her hair and followed the shampoo with an entirely superfluous rinse that promised to "lighten and brighten the dullest hair." And while she was waiting for her hair to dry, she'd given herself a manicure she didn't really need and a pedicure which she did. Especially after hiking over half the island in her flimsy thongs, and even more especially since she intended to wear sandals with the dress.

Darcy could explain all this to herself, however. She could slough it off very easily as a harmless way of passing time till she joined the others for lunch.

What she couldn't explain was that she'd rummaged through her overnight bag for the supply of cosmetics that had remained unopened in the case since Ariel had given it to her two Christmases before.

This was totally out of character for Darcy. Because she seldom used cosmetics, she wasn't very skilled at applying makeup, but after some experimentation, she decided she'd done a fairly creditable job with the eyeshadow and mascara.

The lipstick she wasn't so sure about. One of the reasons she didn't normally wear it was to avoid calling attention to the coquettish shape of her mouth. Now it seemed to her that the lush pink color of the lipstick made her naturally provocative pout appear brazenly enticing, as if she were just waiting for someone to kiss her.

Maybe she should wipe it off.

She was just reaching for a tissue when she caught a glimpse of the rose, which she had carefully arranged in a bud vase on the nightstand.

When she'd gotten home from her walk, the flower had been rather droopy and bedraggled, but it looked a bit perkier now. The deep velvety red of the petals appeared even redder and more velvety by contrast with the vase, which was of eggshell-fine white porcelain.

Seeing this, she began to think that the rose might survive the weekend at that. She fervently hoped it would—but only, she reassured herself, because it was so lovely.

Darcy had glanced back at the mirror when from somewhere in the house she heard the chimes of a clock striking the quarter hour. If the clock was accurate, she was already late for lunch.

With this reminder uppermost in her mind, she picked up her hairbrush instead of the tissue. She ran the brush through her hair several times before she turned away from the mirror and headed decisively for the hall.

Guided by the lilting sound of her mother's laughter, Darcy walked across the lawn. When the terrace came into view, she paused in the shade of an apple tree, studying the group of people gathered there and trying to get her bearings by identifying the other guests.

Set against the dark green backdrop of the pines, the scene that confronted her was a colorful one. It shifted kaleidoscopically as the laughing, chatting people moved about, forming new patterns on their island of soft gray flagstones in the sea of emerald lawn. The men were all nattily turned out, the women wearing bright summer dresses.

She smiled affectionately at the sight of Ariel, willowy and elegant in a gauzy mint green caftan. There was very little gray in Ariel's luxuriant auburn hair, her profile was still striking and her complexion unlined. Ariel, thought Darcy, was like a fine wine. She seemed to improve—to become more beautiful—with age.

Darcy stepped away from the tree, scanning the others in the group as she approached them.

She recognized Jenny Lazenby at first glance. While Ariel was still youthful looking, Jenny was "well preserved." She looked every year of her age, but nicely so. A small woman with doll-like features and tiny hands and feet, Jenny had opted to grow old gracefully. Her delicate bone structure was disguised by a not unpleasing plumpness, and her ample, well-corseted bosom gave her the strutting posture of a pouter pigeon.

Darcy wasn't acquainted with Louis and Yvette Perrigo, but she recognized the couple from the pictures she'd seen of them in magazines and newspapers. Partly because they owned vast tracts of land in California's wine country, and partly because they were a lively and strikingly attractive pair—he tall and blond, she petite and dark—they were the current darlings of the *paparazzi*.

This left only two men on the terrace that Darcy was unable to identify. Seen from a distance, they appeared to be interchangeable. Both were impeccably dressed in white flannel slacks and Lacoste sport shirts. Both were tall and tanned, slender and silver-haired. It was only as she drew nearer that she saw that one of the men was sixtyish while the other was at least twenty years younger.

Darcy had stepped onto the flagstones at the edge of the terrace before she saw Jordan, but when she did see him, she realized she'd been holding her breath and she expelled it in a long sigh.

He hadn't bothered to change his cutoffs or put on any socks, but he was wearing a shirt now. He was lounging on the grass, off to one side, watching the others as if they were figures on a stage, acting out a scene for his personal entertainment.

His casual pose irritated Darcy almost beyond endurance, but she was even more annoyed because he was every bit as sexy as she'd thought this morning.

Who was he, she wondered. And what was his connection with Jenny Lazenby? Was it possible he was the "gigolo" from whom Ariel was determined to rescue her old friend?

Darcy's breath lodged painfully in her throat at this idea, but she had no more time to think about Jordan because in that moment Ariel saw her and caroled, "At last! My prodigal daughter has arrived."

Darcy barely had time to kiss the petal-soft cheek Ariel offered her before Jenny chimed in.

"Why, so she has! Everyone! I'd like you to meet Darcy Cummins."

The reaction of the others to Jenny's announcement was most peculiar. They interrupted their conversations with a curious abruptness, and in unison, as if they were puppets controlled by a common string, their heads turned in Darcy's direction.

Darcy was accustomed to being stared at. Nine times out of ten it was because she was with her mother, and the tenth it was because the person who was staring at her was wondering if her hair was its natural color. But she was not used to being stared at en masse—not so openly, and most assuredly not on a social occasion such as this.

Stirring uncomfortably beneath the battery of eyes, Darcy stammered weakly, "H-hello, everyone."

The spell that held them immobile was broken, but what ensued was even worse. The younger of the two silver-haired men left the Perrigos to rush toward her.

"By God, Ariel!" he shouted. "Where have you been hiding your daughter? She's *perfect* for the job." Grabbing a fistful of Darcy's hair, he brandished it at Louis Perrigo and exclaimed, "Look at that color. Just *look* at it!"

"Most unusual," Louis acceded. He bent over Darcy

to examine the silky silver-gold of her hair more closely before he glanced at Ariel and queried, "It's not out of a bottle?"

"No, it is *not!*" Ariel snapped. "And I'll have you know I haven't been hiding her. She hasn't chosen to be in the public eye, and I respect that decision."

Alarmed by the unwanted attention she was receiving, Darcy tried to back away from Louis, but the silver-haired man was still holding onto her hair, and before she could take more than one step, she found herself surrounded.

"The hair is glorious, but she doesn't have blue eyes." Yvette Perrigo's softly accented voice came from somewhere behind Darcy. "I thought we were in accord that blue eyes are essential."

"We were, Yvette," Louis said thoughtfully. "But now that I've seen her, I'm not so sure. See how her dark eyes emphasize her blondness."

"Blue-eyed blondes are a dime a dozen," argued the silver-haired man. "Her eyes are the *perfect* color. *Absolutely* perfect."

"Their color isn't out of a bottle, either," Ariel added tartly, still offended by Louis's insinuation that her daughter's hair shade was not natural.

Darcy opened her mouth to protest, but suddenly they were all talking at once, spinning her this way and that, inventorying her physical assets as if she were a prize brood mare.

"Will you look at that mouth! It's scrumptious!" the silver-haired man enthused. Despite her confusion, his fondness for hyperbole told Darcy that he must be Miles Bruckner, the Perrigos' expert on advertising.

"But the makeup is crude, *n'est-ce pas?*"

"With that skin, who cares about makeup?"

"She appears to have the figure for it," said Yvette with an impish roll of her eyes. "Such a graceful line from the throat to the bosom! Such a tiny waist!"

"I'd like to see her legs," said Louis Perrigo.

"So would *I,* dear boy. So would I."

This friendly comment came from the older silver-haired man, who, by the process of elimination, must be Harry Templeton. Of all the people crowded around Darcy, he alone seemed to sympathize with her near panic. He smiled at her consolingly and even gave her a conspiratorial wink but the others were outrageous. Briefly, she considered kicking Miles in the shins and making a run for it, but instead she decided to let the comedy continue. Part of her wanted to see just how far these people would carry their astonishing behavior.

"That dress is horrible," said Yvette. "Peasant styles are so—so common!"

"The color's not bad on her, though. Can't you just see her in something fine and gold and shimmery? Something floaty and diaphanous? But not too loose! It should cling. It should suggest. It should *promise*—"

"But of course! Above all else, it should be *distingué.* We want to display the figure, but we must always, *always,* be subtle about it."

"With the right makeup, she just might do," said Louis.

"But does she photograph well?" wondered Yvette.

"Certainly she does," Ariel answered peevishly. "She's *my* daughter, isn't she?"

"Has she ever done any modeling?"

"No, she hasn't, but she's a natural actress."

"How about dancing lessons?" Louis persisted.

"She took some ballet when she was a little girl."

"That's better than nothing, I suppose."

Darcy listened in amazement to this rapid-fire dialogue. She couldn't believe the way they addressed all questions to Ariel, as if she couldn't speak for herself. She was about to do just that when she changed her mind. First she wanted to find out what this was all about.

"I'm sure she'll be perfect, Louis," said Miles rather pompously. "One assumes you approached my agency because you value my judgment in these matters. I'm the one with his finger on the public pulse, and in *my* opinion, she's absolutely perfect!"

Unswayed by Miles Bruckner's show of confidence, Louis said, "I'd like to see her move. And I'd have to see some pictures of her. I'd feel better if I knew for sure she's photogenic."

"That's only natural," said Miles. "I don't expect you to sign her to a long-term contract on the spot! Since she would become the symbol of Perrigo Vineyards, I'd be the first to advise you to exercise caution. We could arrange a photo session with Jere Winston as early as next week."

Louis shook his head. "Even that implies a certain commitment, my friend. After the fiasco with the last model you recommended, I will not be stampeded."

"Perhaps we should avail ourselves of an outside opinion," Yvette interjected. "Jordan's, for instance."

While everyone was looking expectantly at Jordan, Darcy took advantage of their distraction. Redoubling her efforts, she managed to pry her hair out of Miles Bruckner's grasp, though not without pain. When she wriggled free of the crowd, she instinctively darted toward Jordan.

She was so infuriated that she had covered most of the distance separating them before reason returned. That the others had deferred to Jordan, that they had put the decision about whatever it was they were contemplating in *his* hands, was the last straw! She skidded to a stop not three feet away from him and whirled to face her tormentors.

"What's *wrong* with you people? You're acting like a—like a mob!" At a loss for words, she sputtered, "I don't know *when* I've been so angry! Will all of you please stop treating me like a piece of merchandise! And while you're at it, you can also stop talking about me as if I'm not even here!"

Her show of temper was followed by a stunned silence. Jenny went pink with embarrassment, Ariel was wearing an exaggeratedly innocent expression that seemed to say "Who, me?", the Perrigos were rather shamefaced, and Miles Bruckner was shifting from one foot to the other and studying the toes of his shoes.

As for Jordan, he sprang lightly to his feet, panto-mimed a few boxing jabs, and said, "Go get 'em, Darcy! The smart money's on you to win by a knockout."

Some of the stiffness left Darcy's spine, but it was Harry Templeton who finally smoothed over the tension.

"So, Louis," he said, his eyes twinkling wickedly, "at least now you've had the opportunity to see Darcy move."

"And she moves very gracefully, if I may say so," Louis complimented.

With an elfin smile Yvette amended, "We've also learned she has lovely carriage and a great deal of sang-froid."

But Darcy was not to be mollified so easily. With a disdainful toss of her head, she retorted, "Sangfroid, indeed! I don't think I've ever felt *less* self-possessed than I do right now. What's more, Madame Perrigo, I'll bet that even you would be a trifle upset if you'd been mauled about by a bunch of total strangers—"

"Ah, Dar-cee," Yvette interjected huskily. "Louis and I—Miles too—are, all of us, most desolate that we have offended you. But if we have been overeager, it is be-cause for months now we have been looking for a woman with just the right hair, just the right face, just the right figure for our advertising campaign. Perrigo's is going nationwide, you see, and we must capture the public favor—"

"It's going to be really big," Miles Bruckner broke in enthusiastically. "The biggest thing since—since Chi-quita Banana! We're planning a series of ads in maga-zines, on television, and billboards—"

"So perhaps you can understand how crucial it is that we find the right model," said Yvette. "Please, Dar-cee, will you forgive us?"

Yvette's gracious apology won Darcy over, especially because of the new piquancy the Frenchwoman had given her name by accenting the last syllable. Besides, once Darcy had vented her temper, she'd always found it hard to stay angry.

"How can I not forgive you, madame," she relented, smiling, "when you pronounce my name so charmingly?"

"We are friends, then?"

Bemused by the emergence of Yvette's sunny smile when only seconds before she had seemed on the verge of tears, Darcy nodded.

"Formidable! Then you won't mind if Jordan answers our question?"

"Your question, madame?"

"As to whether you, Dar-cee, are the very young woman we have been searching for these many months."

"No, madame. I honestly don't see the point, but I suppose there's no real harm in that."

Darcy could only assume that all eyes were focused upon Jordan once again. He certainly dominated her own attention; so much so that she forgot about the others. And from the intent way he studied her, his bold blue eyes wandering over her in frank assessment, there might have been just the two of them standing on that sunlit patch of lawn beside the terrace.

"First I want to file a disclaimer," he began slowly. "I don't believe in giving advice. Generally speaking, even when someone asks for it, they don't want it, unless you tell them what they want to hear. Furthermore, I don't know much about advertising, and I know even less about wine. There have been times when I've thought I was an expert on women—"

"Hear, hear!"

Jordan acknowledged Harry Templeton's cheer with a slight inclination of his head and continued speaking as if without interruption.

". . . and there have been other times when I've *known* I'm not an expert about women or anything else, so I can only give you my views as a man. Am I making myself clear, Louis?"

"Most definitely," said Louis, laughing a bit. "Please, Jordan, go on."

"Well then, to give my candid opinion, Darcy has a magnificent body and remarkable hair. She's attractive enough to turn on the average man and ladylike enough that wives won't feel she's a threat to their happy homes." A smile tugged at one corner of his mouth and danced in his eyes. "She is also rather short to be a model, but I'm sure if she puts her mind to it, she can figure out some way to fake some extra height."

Was that *all* he intended to say about her, Darcy wondered as she watched Jordan walking toward the serving cart, where an assortment of wine bottles was chilling in individual ice buckets.

She hardly knew whether she'd been damned with faint praise or sincerely complimented. The way he'd said "magnificent body" seemed more insolent than flattering, and "remarkable" was a somewhat ambiguous adjective for her hair. There was something so infuriatingly condescending in his tone as he spoke of her— as if he wanted to remind her that he'd seen her at her most vulnerable that night at Santino's.

He had also, she reminded herself, overestimated her resourcefulness. All of her adult life she'd wished she were taller than five feet four, but so far she hadn't been able to come up with a way of "faking it."

Although she felt let down and strangely abandoned, Darcy remained where she was, but the others clustered around Jordan as he read the labels on the wine bottles. He discarded several bottles of Perrigo champagne before he found one that appealed to him.

"Ah, yes," he remarked to no one in particular. "I've heard that this was a very good year."

"An excellent choice," Louis affirmed.

Peeling back the foil wrapper, Jordan expertly uncorked the bottle and poured the champagne into tulip-shaped crystal glasses that Louis helped him distribute. When everyone had been served, Jordan held out his hand to Darcy.

She went to him automatically, but even if she'd thought about it, she would have been powerless to resist him. When she reached his side, he put his arm around her waist and pulled her close to his side—so close that she could feel the hard imprint of his thigh through the fabric of her dress. And from that point of contact came an ever-increasing excitement that spread like wildfire through her veins, igniting long-dormant impulses until it seemed to Darcy that she was being consumed by her desire for this man.

Was Jordan aware of her reaction to him? Did he know that she was trembling inside?

It seemed terribly important that he shouldn't guess the effect he was having on her and, recalling the ease with which he could read her thoughts, she averted her face and concentrated on the bubbles floating upward in the hollow stem of her wineglass, counting them as they rose to the surface.

She looked up in surprise as Jordan raised his own glass and said, "Ladies and gentlemen, I give you Perrigo's 'Champagne Blonde'!"

Good Lord! thought Darcy. *He's referring to me!*

"To the success of our campaign," said Louis.

Only Jordan noticed that she didn't drink Louis's toast. In a voice meant for her ears alone, he muttered, "Now all you have to do is convince Darcy to cooperate."

Chapter 4

FOR THE THIRD time in as many minutes Darcy knocked at the door of Ariel's bedroom. When there was no response, she pressed her ear against the paneling of the door and stood there silently, listening for any sound that might give away her mother's presence.

"Ariel's not in there."

Startled by Jordan's husky drawl, Darcy spun around to see him standing just behind her.

"Your mother and my aunt are in the den, playing bridge with Harry and Miles."

Jordan moved a step closer, blocking everything else from view with his wide shoulders, filling her senses just as he seemed to fill the hall. Darcy's heart skipped a beat and one hand rushed to conceal the pulses that were hammering in her throat.

"Must you sneak up on me like that? You scared me half to death!"

"It wasn't intentional," Jordan said dryly. "I'm sure you'll agree it's not easy to give warning when you're walking on carpeting with deck shoes."

Irritated by his unshakable calm, Darcy asked abruptly, "What are you doing here, anyway?"

"I don't need an excuse. Didn't Ariel mention to you that I own the place?"

"My mother didn't mention it, but Harry Templeton did. He filled me in on quite a few things."

Jordan nodded. "I noticed you two were talking nonstop at lunch."

"Harry was most informative," said Darcy. "He told me that you're Jenny's nephew and that Miles Bruckner is one of her ex-husbands—"

"He was her second," Jordan cut in, "and although Aunt Jen's been married and divorced twice since they split up, she still has a soft spot in her heart for good old Miles. She's always been true to him in her fashion. When they were divorced, she set him up in his agency, and now she's doing everything she can to see that he makes a go of it."

"That's one reason I want to talk to my mother," Darcy said grimly. "She claimed she couldn't come to Seattle this weekend because your aunt needed her. She said Jenny was about to remarry and the consequences could be disastrous. Not only that, she led me to believe that Harry Templeton was the worst kind of opportunist. I ask you, can you imagine a less likely villain?"

"In all fairness to Ariel, she might have gotten the wrong impression about Harry. Aunt Jenny does not have a terrific track record where men are concerned, and Ariel's been through a lot with her."

"So Mother said, but even so, I'm almost certain she got me here under false pretenses. It wouldn't be the first time, and after meeting Harry, no one could believe he's the cad she made him out to be. He and Jenny seem to be genuinely fond of each other, and he swears they're not planning marriage. Even if they were, I don't think he'd be any threat to her."

"No, he wouldn't," Jordan agreed. "Harry makes no secret of the fact that he was quite an operator in his younger years, but he strikes me as comparatively harmless nowadays."

In her frustration Darcy pounded the side of her fist against the doorjamb and cried, "It drives me up the wall when Ariel pulls a stunt like this!" Smiling ruefully, she added, "I suppose I should apologize for snapping at you when it's really her I'm angry with. She knows she owes me an explanation, and since she doesn't have one, her solution is to avoid me."

"And she's likely to go on avoiding you till you've had a chance to cool off."

"It's obvious you know her well."

"Let's just say that I've seen both her and my aunt in action often enough to know how much they enjoy remaking the world to conform to their standards."

"If you know all that, maybe *you* can tell me why my mother maneuvered me into coming here. Was it because of the Perrigos' advertising campaign?"

"I doubt it. Ariel is a superb actress, but when they pounced on you, she seemed genuinely surprised."

"Then why?" Darcy asked. "What was so important that Mother insisted I join her this weekend?"

"Think about it," Jordan directed her pointedly, leaning against the wall with one ankle casually hooked over the other.

The smooth rippling of the muscles in his shoulders, the bunching of his biceps when he folded his arms across his chest, made it clear that his indolence was a pose. No one could stay so hard and fit without regular workouts. And his finely chiseled mouth belied the aggressive set of his jaw.

His mouth, Darcy thought, betrayed a nature that was both sensitive and sensuous. It was made for smiling—

or for kissing. Under Ariel's rating system, that alone would earn him a 9.5.

Realization dawned with electrifying swiftness.

"My God!" she gasped. "It was all arranged so we could meet, wasn't it?"

"You've got it, Goldilocks," Jordan said breezily. "My aunt and your mother have been plotting to bring us together for years."

Darcy shook her head as if to deny her own logic. "But Mother's never once mentioned you to me!"

"If she had, how would you have reacted?" Jordan must have read the answer to his question in the way her eyes shied away from his. "You'd never have come to Roche Harbor willingly, would you, Darcy?" he said softly. "Ariel would have had to hogtie you to get you here."

"You're right, of course," Darcy confessed. "No offense intended."

"None taken."

She stole a glance at him and their eyes met and locked. Darcy felt a dizzying weakness in her knees and clung to the doorjamb in the hope that Jordan wouldn't detect his overpowering effect on her. "And were you in on this little scheme, or was subterfuge necessary to get you here for the weekend, too?"

"As a matter of fact," he answered steadily, "the ostensible reason I was included in the party was that I'd promised to let Louis and Miles take a look at my boat. It seems they're considering shooting one of their commercials aboard a sailboat and—well, as I said, Aunt Jen's determined to see that Miles's agency is successful. But if Aunt Jen had informed me you were going to be here, I'd have come anyway," he added. "I mean, Jenny's tried to fix me up before, although I must say, her taste is improving."

"Thank you, kind sir," she replied facetiously. "To return the compliment, my mother could have chosen worse."

Jordan beamed at her approvingly. "I'm glad you're such a good sport, Darcy."

"Well," she replied crisply, "great expectations seem to be riding on this weekend. What do you suppose we do about them?"

Jordan's low chuckle brought back all too vividly their encounter at Santino's. "You really *are* a good sport, Goldilocks," he affirmed. "My suggestion is to play along. That might keep Jenny and Ariel off our backs."

"What do you mean by playing along?" Darcy asked cautiously.

"Jen and Ariel are too smart to be taken in unless we put on a good show," Jordan replied. "So for openers, I think we should spend the next day and a half totally absorbed with each other. And what the hell! If you're up to it, we could even act like we're serious and continue to date in Seattle. Then, after a believable length of time has gone by—or whenever it's convenient to either of us to break it off—we can tell them we've discovered we're not compatible after all. What do you think?"

"I think that we don't have to commit ourselves beyond this weekend."

Although Darcy had answered coolly, she was shocked by how appealing Jordan's plan was. His nonchalance was ego deflating. He'd made it clear that the romantic scenario he'd concocted was strictly for Jenny and Ariel's benefit. But at least he had honestly let her know where she stood. If she went along with his scheme, there would be no misunderstandings or hurt feelings.

Moreover, he had a point about getting the two matchmakers off their backs. If she rejected Jordan without seeming to give him a chance, Ariel would immediately come up with another candidate—and another and another. However, if she gave the appearance of being enamored with Jordan, then announced that their relationship hadn't worked out, Ariel might be sufficiently chastened to let her daughter manage her own social life in the future.

The truth was, Darcy silently conceded, Jordan's plan was more than appealing. For some indefinable reason, the thought of being with him was downright irresistible!

"In other words," she said, "since we're thrown together here anyway, I agree to our making a show of interest in each other for the moment. As for the long term—well, why don't we play it by ear?"

"A sporting answer, Goldilocks," Jordan returned equably. "What do you say we begin showing our good faith right now? I'm on my way to move my boat to a new mooring. Why don't you come with me? If you'd like, we could even go for a sail."

If she'd like! Darcy couldn't think of anything she'd like better. As long as they both understood they were assuming roles to placate Ariel and Jenny, the whole episode might be an amusing diversion.

Ariel had accused her often enough of being a frustrated actress. Now, with Jordan's cooperation, she had a crack at a plum part.

"Jordan," she replied in a throaty murmur that would have melted Rhett Butler's heart, "nothing would give me more pleasure."

Chapter 5

LIKE THE SPIRITED thoroughbred she was, the *Compass Rose* swung at her moorings as if eager to show her heels to the fickle June breezes that whispered across the harbor.

Jordan was boyishly proud of the ketch, and with good reason. The resplendent white of her hull was relieved by a smart, narrow band of black trim that emphasized her sleekness, and from bowsprit to stern, every line of the sailboat was clean, elegant, classic.

"She beats to windward remarkably well for a ketch," Jordan boasted as he rowed the dinghy toward the sailboat, "so well, I'd match her with any boat on the Sound— and she's fitted with the finest electronic gear and completely equipped for single-handed deep-water cruising."

"Have you taken her out on the ocean?" Darcy asked.

"Sure I have. I just returned from a shakedown cruise to Ensenada."

"But she looks so small—"

"Small!" Scowling, Jordan leaped to the defense of his sailboat. "The *Compass Rose* is *compact*, not small! She has two double staterooms with attached heads, a full galley, a dinette, and a salon. She measures forty feet, six inches on deck, twelve feet amidships, and thirty-three feet at the waterline. Her draft is five and a half feet, and she displaces twenty-two thousand pounds. Now, do you still think she's small?"

Chastened, Darcy shook her head. "She really is a beauty, Jordan. What class is she?"

Because of the loving way Jordan's eyes traveled over the sailboat, Darcy was not at all surprised when he answered, "The *Compass Rose* is in a class by herself."

"I'm sure she is," Darcy returned. "But who's her designer?"

"You're looking at him." Jordan chuckled at her look of wide-eyed amazement. "I'm a naval architect by education, a boat builder by occupation, and a sailor by inclination."

"You sound like a folk song!" Darcy laughed, suitably impressed. "How ever did you get to be all those things all at once?"

"I was indoctrinated at an early age. My grandfather had a boatyard, and from the time I learned to walk, I spent as much time with him at the yard as my parents would allow. Grandpop taught me everything he knew about boats, from the ground up, and a boy couldn't have asked for a finer teacher. He never looked upon the boatyard as a business. He cared more about the quality of his product than he did about turning a profit. To him boat-building was a calling—just about the highest calling a man could have—and he was a purist. He was also an artist. Whether he was building a rowboat or a schooner, he'd never deliver a boat to a customer until it met his personal requirements of aesthetics and performance."

"You sound rather wistful," Darcy observed. "Have

things changed so much since your grandfather's day?"

She knew her question had struck a nerve before Jordan answered. He applied himself to the oars with a fury that expressed his discontent with the status quo more eloquently than words.

"Haven't you heard?" he said. "We're living in the age of specialization, where the object is to know more and more about less and less. I've done my damndest not to become slipshod, but I've had to treat the boatyard like a business to keep it from going under."

Not knowing how to respond to Jordan's indictment, Darcy trailed one hand in the water and concentrated on the scenery.

The pristine white steeple of Our Lady of Good Voyage Chapel was just barely visible above the leafy green treetops of the hillside. It reached reverently toward the blue of the heavens as if it were beseeching divine benediction. Below the chapel, the village of Roche Harbor basked in the hot summer sun, while throngs of tourists strolled about, enjoying the quietly festive Saturday afternoon.

Hundreds of boats were neatly tied up beside the docks and others were strewn at sheltered anchorages about the bay, their colorful burgees shimmering in the heat-haze that danced above the surface of the water.

Seen from her seat in the yacht tender, the town, the harbor, and the marina presented a breathtakingly lovely panorama, but inevitably Darcy's eyes strayed back to Jordan.

Beads of sweat had sprung out on his forehead, and his neck was corded with exertion. She watched him surreptitiously, admiring the supple play of muscles beneath the coppery skin of his chest and the rhythmic pumping of his arms and legs as he propelled the dinghy across the bay.

He was perspiring freely when they reached the *Compass Rose*, and he doused his face with water before he handed her aboard. As he stepped onto the transom, the sudden warmth of a smile erased the harsh lines from his face.

"Sorry about that," he said lightly. "I didn't mean to lecture you."

"That's all right," Darcy replied.

Jordan secured the dinghy at the stern of the ketch and began removing the sail covers.

"You must have loved your grandfather a great deal," she added softly.

The deft movements of Jordan's hands stopped abruptly. He raised his head and stared at some far distant point on the island as if he were staring into the past. For a few seconds he remained immobile, his rugged profile etched against the sky. Then, with a start, he turned to Darcy and acknowledged simply, "Yes, I did. I respected him, too. More than anyone I've ever known."

"Were you named for him?"

Jordan laughed. "Actually, I was named for a woman."

"A woman!" Darcy stared at him incredulously.

"That's right," he said. "Good old Eva Mae Jordan— and I don't use the word *old* lightly!" Jordan smiled reminiscently as he continued: "She must have been eighty when I was born, and she didn't die until five years ago. Since I was twenty-seven at the time, that means she lived to be one hundred and seven!"

Darcy hurried after Jordan when he headed toward the bow of the ketch and began hauling in the bowline hand over hand, pulling the boat toward its mooring buoy.

Her hands on her hips, she cried, "Jordan Ives! You can't leave me in suspense like that. Aren't you going to tell me why your parents named you for Eva Mae? Was she a friend of the family or something?"

"She was a friend, but I'm not sure my folks did it because of that. I think they hoped she'd be so flattered they'd named their only child for her that she'd reciprocate by naming them in her will."

"And did she?"

"Nope. Shrewd woman that she was, Eva Mae out-foxed 'em. She survived my parents by nearly ten years."

Darcy's face grew hot with embarrassment. "I'm sorry," she murmured. "I'm not usually so tactless."

"It all happened a long time ago, so don't let it worry you." Jordan studied her quizzically. "Are you always so uptight, or is it me that's got you on edge?"

"N-no, it's not you." She sighed heavily, wondering if he believed her fib. "It's just that this seems to be my day for making awkward assumptions."

Jordan draped an arm about her shoulders and gave her a reassuring hug. "I like your spontaneity, Goldi-locks," he said. "It's refreshing, and I'll bet you're not awkward about anything. But maybe you could save any other questions till we're under way."

"Oh, yes. Of course!" Flustered by Jordan's compli-ment, by his arm about her shoulders, she chattered on nervously, "We've wasted enough time as it is. I can hardly wait to get started. Can I do anything for you?"

Darcy's question had been straightforward, but Jordan apparently chose to hear a sexual innuendo where none had been intended. A warm glow of intimacy lit the languid blue depths of his eyes as they roved suggestively over her body, lingering as palpably as a fiery caress on the soft curves of her breasts and hips. The atmosphere between them fairly crackled with mutual awareness.

"That depends," he drawled mockingly. "What did you have in mind?"

Darcy's mouth was suddenly dry, and she moistened her lips with the tip of her tongue.

Why had she ever thought she could treat this as a lark, a test of her acting ability? She found it difficult even to think straight when Jordan was near. It had been less than an hour since they'd left the house, and already she had let him catch her off guard.

Even worse was that the way he was looking at her

made her feel tongue-tied. She was trembling. Her wits were in such disarray, she couldn't even begin to come up with an adequate response to his advances.

Finally she decided that he was moving too fast for her, and that honesty might be the best policy.

"I—I can't think of anything clever to say," she admitted feebly.

Jordan must have recognized the entreaty in her voice, for his expression visibly softened. "There are times, Darcy, when directness is much more effective than cleverness," he said gently.

"Is this one of them?"

Jordan smiled wryly. "I think maybe it is."

Darcy drew in a deep, ragged breath. "Well then, since I haven't had much experience with sailing, perhaps you could suggest something I could do to help get under way."

Jordan's expression changed to one of friendly amusement. Handing her the bowline, he teased, "If that's your best offer, you might as well stand by to cast off."

Chapter 6

FOR THE NEXT half-hour Jordan was occupied with hoisting the sails and guiding the *Compass Rose* out of the busy harbor. After she had done her bit by casting off, Darcy worked her way along the deck to the stern of the boat. She sat quietly in the small open cockpit, watching Jordan at the helm and vowing not to lose sight of her reason for being there again.

But all too soon her alert single-mindedness gave way to the purely physical pleasures afforded by the warm caress of the sun and the wind upon her skin and the cooling kiss of the salt spray on her face.

Keeping to the middle of the narrow waterway between Henry and Pearl Islands, they sailed toward the more open water of Speiden Channel. Posey Island came into view off the starboard bow, then Little Barren Island, unique for its desertlike growth of cactus.

The breeze freshened as they rounded McCracken

Point, and Jordan brought the *Compass Rose* about, setting a course that would let them run with the wind along the western shore of Henry Island. Minutes later, the Anacortes ferry appeared to stern, trailing half a dozen kites that were being flown from its upper deck by commuters bound for British Columbia. Jordan and Darcy laughed together at the cheerful sight.

Now that they were in Haro Strait, they had more room to maneuver, and Jordan relaxed a bit at the wheel. He rubbed the back of his neck and slouched deeper into the cushion that padded the bench. Stretching out one arm along the lifeline behind him, he half turned toward Darcy and offered politely, "There's some beer and soda in the galley if you'd care for a cold drink."

"I could go for that," said Darcy. When Jordan started to get up, she jumped to her feet. "Let me do the honors," she volunteered. "I'd really like to see the cabin."

Jordan grinned, obviously delighted at her display of interest in the boat. "Okay," he agreed.

Darcy slid back the hatch at the top of the companionway. "What would you like to drink?" she asked.

"I'll have a beer, but take your time. Look around all you want."

Taking Jordan at his word, Darcy did some exploring before she fetched the drinks. She bypassed the navigation station out of cautious respect for its sophisticated array of electronic gear and went into the galley. It was well equipped and obviously planned for efficiency. There was not an inch of wasted space, and, despite its smallness, it was bright and cheery.

The mahogany-paneled salon and staterooms, on the other hand, were surprisingly roomy. The master stateroom was especially luxurious, fitted with built-in lockers and a spacious double berth that had been designed to accommodate Jordan's big frame.

Everything about the boat was meticulously neat. There was not a wrinkle to mar the smoothness of the quilted burgundy corduroy bedspread. The brightwork glistened, the paneling was polished to a high gloss, and the pillows on the sofa in the salon had been arranged with an almost mathematical precision that spoke of the lavish attention Jordan gave to the *Compass Rose*.

Darcy was deep in thought as she took two beers from the refrigerator in the galley. She started to climb the companionway ladder, then at the last second she decided to return to the galley, left the cans of beer on the counter, and went into one of the heads to check her appearance in the mirror.

Before they'd left the house, she had changed into white linen slacks and a close-fitting red-and-white striped pullover, both of which emphasized her slim but curvaceous figure. Most of the makeup she had applied so carefully before lunch had mysteriously vanished, but that was probably just as well, because exposure to the sun and wind had enhanced her natural color. Her cheeks were vividly pink and her hazel eyes were gold-flecked and sparkling with excitement beneath the sweep of her lashes. If she'd only stop second-guessing Jordan at every turn, she might enjoy this excursion after all. The *Compass Rose* really was impressive, and Jordan obviously responded to her appreciation of it. As she collected the frost-beaded cans from the galley and returned topside, Darcy resolved to relax and enjoy herself.

"You're looking mighty pleased about something," Jordan observed as she handed him his beer.

"It's your boat!" Darcy exclaimed, thankful that she could honestly praise the ketch. "She really is terrific. I love the way the galley's arranged, and everything is so beautifully finished!"

Jordan studied her intently for a moment, then looked away to survey the set of the sails and the unbroken expanse of cobalt sea that lay dead ahead of the *Compass Rose*. After taking a long swallow of beer, he remarked, "You said you'd done some sailing."

"Enough to know that you were right when you said the *Compass Rose* sails like a dream," Darcy replied earnestly. "The summer I was eleven, my father chartered a sloop and we cruised north from Vancouver, in the Strait of Georgia."

"How did you like it?"

"It was wonderful. In fact, it was one of the nicest times my father and I ever had together. I remember one night we anchored in a little inlet where the beaches were literally paved with oysters. You couldn't take a step without treading on one. Anyway, I took the dinghy ashore and in five minutes I was back on board with a bucketful for our dinner. My father was terribly impressed, but he did something that at the time impressed me even more."

Smiling indulgently, Jordan prompted, "What was that?"

"He shucked one of the oysters and ate it—raw! I couldn't have been more surprised if he'd suddenly sprouted wings and flown."

Darcy paused to drink some of her beer. Then she mused, "It's funny, the things we remember. My father died only two months after that, but my clearest memory of that summer is the way he ate that oyster."

"Were you close to him?"

She took another sip of beer. "To be honest, not very. Daddy was fifty when I was born, and I guess that's kind of late in life to start learning how to be a father. Whatever the reason, we weren't very comfortable with each other. Oh, I never doubted that he loved me, but he always seemed—I don't know—distant somehow. Mother says it was my doing as much as his. She says I tended to put him on a pedestal."

"And is she right about that?"

"I don't know," Darcy replied uncertainly. "Probably. My mother usually is right about me." Faltering into silence, she gave herself a mental shake and added, "I don't know why I'm telling you all this. It must be the beer talking. Anyway, I'd much rather hear about you.

Would you tell me about some of the sailing you've done?"

She was relieved when Jordan readily complied with her request. It was almost as if he were trying to put her at ease. And she didn't have to pretend an interest as he spoke of crewing on a friend's boat in a recent TransPac race, of sailing from Hawaii through the South Pacific before they came home.

He talked at some length about visits to Polynesian towns whose very names evoked images of a tropical paradise. He told her about Papeete, Pago Pago, and Nouméa. He described hot, lazy days and cool, star-kissed nights. He tried to convey the peace he'd felt when caught up in the rhythm of the sea. She laughed until her sides ached at one anecdote he told about the rowdy initiation he'd undergone on the occasion of his first crossing of the equator.

Captivated by Jordan's stories, Darcy barely noticed that they had passed the southernmost tip of Henry Island and were sailing along the coast of San Juan Island again, gently ghosting in a zigzag course as they threaded their way through the fjordlike inlet that led back to Roche Harbor. Since they were in the lee of Henry Island, there was very little wind, and the stately ranks of evergreens that studded the shore were reflected in the cool, still water.

An escort of gulls and cormorants flew in ever-widening circles in the sky above the *Compass Rose,* while a pair of curious harbor seals frolicked in the wake of the boat. Occasionally, one of the seals would swim alongside, appearing and disappearing in a rainbow arc of sleekness. When Jordan sailed the *Compass Rose* into Garrison Bay, the seals followed, but when he lowered the jib, they dove out of sight, perhaps alarmed by the flurry of activity on board the ketch.

Jordan sheeted in the mizzen and held it flat to keep the bow into the wind while he picked up a mooring buoy. When the *Compass Rose* was anchored and the mizzen sail reefed, he called to Darcy, "How about a swim?"

"Sounds great!"

Scooping up her beach bag, she started toward the cabin. Although she was eager to be in the water, Darcy took her time changing. Her maillot bathing suit was cut fairly high on the hip, but it was modest enough when dry. When it was wet, however, the blue and lilac floral-printed lycra clung to her like a second skin, leaving very little of her body to the imagination.

Jordan was already in the water when she climbed back on deck. She struck a graceful pose by the rope ladder on the transom, but he was swimming away from the boat and never even glanced her way. She waited until he turned and swam in her direction, but he still didn't look at her.

Finally, Darcy abandoned her Esther Williams role. Rising onto her tiptoes and springing high above the deck, she wrapped her arms tightly around her knees and caromed into the water, landing nearly on top of Jordan in a noisy, splashing cannonball. But all this earned her was a shocking numbness as the icy water enveloped her sun-warmed flesh.

She came up sputtering. "M-my God! It's f-f-freezing! Why d-didn't you warn me?"

"You didn't give me time, so I'd say you got what you deserved." Jordan shook the water out of his eyes and grinned mischievously. "How old did you say you are, little girl?"

"I didn't," she replied through chattering teeth.

She was treading water, watching Jordan swim away from her again, when something warm and furry brushed against her thigh. Squealing with fright, Darcy thrashed about and began kicking toward the beach, increasing the pace of her crawl stroke when the creature bumped into her a second time.

She tried to call Jordan, but her teeth were now chattering so badly that she was almost mute. She was also bordering on terror, and she swam even faster.

At the third contact with the creature she saw a flashing streak of silvery-brown break the surface of the water. Her fear began to ebb, and when she dove under to investigate, she found herself staring into a pair of luminous brown eyes. Her playful companion, she discovered, was one of the harbor seals.

Delighted, she reached out to pet the seal, but he darted away, and now it was she who pursued the seal, swimming as fast as she could and trying to imitate his graceful underwater acrobatics until she was forced to return to the surface for air.

After she'd caught her breath, she hailed Jordan. By now she was used to the chill of the water and her voice carried far enough that he heard her. When he stopped swimming and turned toward her, she gestured at the seal, who was turning slow somersaults beside her, waiting for her to rejoin him.

"Look what I found!" she called merrily.

"I see you have a playmate." Jordan chuckled. Still smiling at the antics of the seal, he ducked underwater and swam toward them.

The next half-hour was one of the most enchanting Darcy had ever experienced. Jordan and she romped with the seal through the crystal-clear waters of the bay. Weaving in and out among the rocky shoals in the shallows, they played a hectic game of hide-and-seek with the friendly little animal.

After a while the other seal appeared, and the four of them moved to deeper water for an aquatic version of tag until, at last, tiring of the sport, the two seals swam away.

Darcy dove under and tried to follow after them, but within a very short distance she was forced to give up the chase. Her arms and legs were leaden and her lungs burned with the need for air.

When she surfaced this time, she swam desultorily

toward the beach. Just as her feet touched the sandy bottom, a powerboat nudged its hesitant way into the cove, and she stood up in the hip-deep water to watch its approach.

As the cabin cruiser drew nearer, Darcy saw that a woman was at the wheel. Dark-haired, deeply tanned, and attractive, she was wearing a minuscule bikini that revealed most of her buxom figure.

"Hello," she called to Darcy. Jordan surfaced nearby just then, rising from the water like some pagan sea god, and the woman repeated with a new, almost lecherous emphasis, "Well, *hello!*"

Jordan raked his hair out of his eyes with one hand. "Hi there," he replied genially.

The woman eyed him avidly as she confessed, "I hate to admit it, but I have absolutely no sense of direction. I'm afraid I'm lost. Is this Mitchell Bay?"

"This is Garrison Bay," said Jordan. "Mitchell Bay is the next one south."

"I see." Although she had the information she'd come for, the woman made no move to leave. She was practically leering at Jordan as she asked, "Have you done much sailing around here?"

"A fair amount," he replied.

She pointed toward the *Compass Rose*. "Is that your sailboat?"

"Yes, it is."

"Well, aren't you the lucky one, owning such a gorgeous boat! I've always wanted to try sailing myself, but George—that's my hubby—says he doesn't have time to wait around for the wind to blow."

"Maybe someday you'll get him to change his mind."

"Believe me, I've tried, but no luck so far." The woman leaned over the gunnel of the cruiser, pillowing her voluptuous breasts on her forearm and giving Jordan a better view of her cleavage. "Tell me," she said confidentially, "is it hard to stand up on one of those things when the deck gets all slanty?"

"You mean when the boat heels over?"

The woman smiled at Jordan warmly. "I guess that's what they call it."

"Most of the time it's not too hard. We do our best to keep the deck from getting too—uh, slanty."

"How interesting!"

When Jordan made no response to this, the woman glanced at her wristwatch and reluctantly said, "I really should be going. I'm late as it is, and George hates it when I'm late. If you're coming into Friday Harbor for the night, why don't you—and your little friend too, of course—join George and me for cocktails? We're staying at the Lonesome Cove."

"That's very nice of you, but we're on our way into Roche Harbor. I've reserved a berth in Nelson Bay."

The woman's face fell. She lingered for several more minutes before she ran out of conversational gambits. Finally, she turned the nose of the powerboat toward the mouth of the bay and gunned the motor. As the boat picked up speed, she waved airily and called, "See you around sometime."

"Sure, see you," Jordan replied.

He followed the craft with his gaze, measuring its seaworthiness with an expert's eyes until it had disappeared beyond the point.

"What did you think of her?" asked Darcy.

"She's a little beamy," Jordan said absently.

Darcy laughed. "I meant the owner, not the boat!"

Grinning, Jordan repeated, "She's a little beamy."

Darcy wrinkled her nose at him. "Then you didn't find her attractive?"

"Yes, she's attractive, but I prefer women whose lines are a little racier." He turned toward Darcy and his eyes roamed slowly over her body. "You, for instance, are very nicely balanced. I'd say you're about thirty-five inches on deck, twenty-four amidships, and thirty-four at the waterline."

Sending a splash of water toward Jordan's laughing

face, Darcy cried, "Jordan Ives, you're incorrigible!"

"Ah, but am I right?" he persisted, undaunted.

"You're close, but I don't think I like being described in nautical terms."

"Why not? Women and boats aren't dissimilar."

"Oh?"

"Seriously, why do you think it's traditional to refer to boats as females?"

"Because some male chauvinist started the tradition?" Darcy suggested pertly.

"Not at all," Jordan countered, straight-faced. "It's because boats are like women in so many ways. Both should be trim. Both should carry enough ballast to give them stability when the going gets rough, but not so much that they lose their natural buoyancy, otherwise they won't be lively enough. And the best of them don't make too many waves, but even then they require constant attention if you hope to keep them in line—"

Darcy interrupted Jordan's comparison by splashing him again, and this time he retaliated. Diving toward her, he caught her up in his arms and waded out to deeper water, carrying her with him. She kicked and squirmed halfheartedly, but he easily tightened his hold on her wriggling form.

"Don't you want to hear the rest?" he teased.

By now Darcy was laughing uncontrollably. She was also winded from her struggles. She didn't sound very convincing even to her own ears as she replied, "I think I've heard quite enough, thank you."

"But I saved the best for last!"

Without warning, Jordan removed the arm that supported her knees and her legs drifted downward, allowing him to fasten both arms around her waist. Their bodies bumped, then floated together lightly, then met and clung in a liquid fusion of flesh as Jordan lifted her higher in the water, holding her against his broad chest so that their eyes were on the same level and their mouths were the merest fraction of an inch apart.

Mesmerized by the smoky blue of his eyes, Darcy linked her arms around his neck, and he pressed her soft, slippery body even closer to his masculine hardness.

His breath sighed across her face as he said, "Women and boats are alike in that both of them should be responsive to the lightest touch."

As if to prove his point, before the whisper of his voice had completely died away, Jordan touched his mouth lightly to hers. The taste of the sea on his lips became indistinguishable from the saltiness of her own lips as he kissed her softly, sweetly.

When he raised his head, he smiled at her almost tenderly. "Miles was right," he murmured. "Your mouth *is* scrumptious."

He rubbed his cheek against hers and her pulses thudded wildly. Her heart was beating so loudly, she was sure he must be able to hear it as he began scattering a tantalizing barrage of kisses over her eyelids, her cheeks, her earlobes, the side of her neck. She was breathless with anticipation when, at last, his mouth returned to hers. His lips brushed hers coaxingly from side to side, and when her own lips softened beneath his gentle insistence, his kiss became frankly erotic. Now he was seeking, asking, compelling, robbing her of the last remnants of resistance to him.

Her body went slack, yielding to his embrace, even as her hands revealed the total abandon of her response to him. She wove her fingers through his hair and ran them over his back, relishing the rough texture of his hair, learning the substance and shape of his shoulder blades, discovering the way his muscles flexed and the smoothness of his water-slicked skin.

Her lips parted eagerly, enticing the hungry penetration of his tongue, welcoming this intimacy—wanting it—and they kissed lingeringly and demandingly, not at all softly, but even more sweetly.

Both of them were trembling when they moved apart. Jordan's eyes were widely dilated and his face was taut and dark with passion. Her fingertips dug into his shoulders as she drew him toward her, and they kissed a third time, harder and more deeply than before, as if they were starved for each other.

One of his hands was tangled in her hair, possessively cradling the base of her skull, while his free hand wandered slowly, knowingly, over her body. The burning warmth of his hand seeped through the fabric of her bathing suit so that she felt branded by his touch when he cupped her breast in his palm. He stroked her nipple with the ball of his thumb, drawing it into a tender bud. Then he teased the bud with his fingertips, cherishing its ripeness until her breasts were engorged and tingling.

A shaky moan escaped her and she clung to him mindlessly as his hand slipped lower, gliding silkily over her rib cage, molding itself to the curve of her waist and the hollow of her spine, exploring the graceful swell of her hips, her neatly rounded derriere, the gentle taper of her thighs, the sensitive plain of her abdomen. But when his fingers touched the velvety skin of her inner thighs and his kiss assumed an even greater urgency, a warning bell clamored shrilly in her head.

She pushed away from him dazedly. She was afraid he might not release her, that he might be angry at her sudden withdrawal, but he only smiled cryptically and swam away from her, striking out toward the *Compass Rose* with his easy overhand crawl.

After some hesitation Darcy also swam toward the boat. The late afternoon sun was hot, but she was shivering when she climbed the rope ladder to the transom.

Jordan was waiting for her in the cockpit, a thick beach towel in his hands. Without a word he wrapped the towel around her and began massaging her shoulders and back to warm her.

From the way he was grinning, she expected him to make some self-congratulatory comment about what had happened between them. She tensed, waiting for him to rub it in that, with her cooperation, he'd proved his assertion that boats and women had certain traits in common—at least this boat and this woman.

She might not want to, but she responded to his lightest touch just as the *Compass Rose* did. Even now, despite the thickness of the terry cloth that separated his hands from the bare skin of her back, his touch was unbearably sensuous.

But when Jordan spoke, he said simply, "I like your bathing suit, Darcy. I like what's in it, too."

For a moment he held her close. His hands moved over her, outlining the curves from hip to waist to breast, and her heart accelerated to a rapid staccato beneath his touch. Then he gave her an affectionate pat on the fanny and moved away from her. He dropped down onto the deck and stretched out on the towel he'd spread there, resting his tawny head on folded arms.

As he closed his eyes, Jordan added calmly, "I'd like very much to make love to you, Darcy."

If his ardor of a few minutes ago had given her cause for concern, his restraint now was even more disquieting. She envied his ability to treat the subject of their making love so lightly. She also resented it.

"At the risk of sounding behind the times," she began stiffly, "I'll be frank with you, Jordan. Before I could go to bed with anyone, I'd have to feel committed—"

"You don't have to explain," Jordan cut in dismissively. "Just let me know if you change your mind."

More confused than before, Darcy spread her own towel on the deck only a few inches away from Jordan's and dropped down beside him. She tried to lie back and relax, but her racing mind wouldn't let her. Her thoughts were in a turmoil. After several minutes had passed, she turned onto her side and studied Jordan.

He was obviously about to fall asleep. His breathing was deep and even, and his hard, craggy features were softened by drowsiness. The unruly lock of hair was flopping over his forehead, and she had to fight against the urge to brush it back.

One of his arms was extended toward her so that his hand was very close to her face, and she shifted her attention to that. Even in repose, even with the long, sun-browned fingers curled back into the palm, his hand was strong and capable looking. She had only to look at it and she remembered the way he'd touched her . . .

Her gaze skidded back to his face. He looked oddly vulnerable with his eyes closed, and she felt a warm rush of tenderness for him. Her throat ached with an emotion she was afraid to define.

She stirred restlessly, mentally casting about for distraction. Perhaps if they talked . . .

"Jordan." She said his name softly.

"Hmmm?" He sounded barely awake.

"Why did you say what you did about the advertising campaign?"

He sighed deeply. "I said several things about it, Darcy. Which one do you mean?"

"You seemed to take it for granted that I wouldn't agree to do the modeling for it. I just wondered why."

Rolling onto his side, Jordan propped his head with one hand and looked at her searchingly. "I just have a gut feeling you wouldn't be happy in that kind of work."

"How can you be sure of that? Are you an authority on modeling?"

"Of course not," Jordan replied evenly, "but I used to date a woman who's a model, and you don't seem the type for it."

His statement that he'd once dated a model made Darcy regret she'd brought up the subject. *Dated* was a word that might be applied to any sort of relationship, from the most platonic to the most intimate. Naturally, she'd assumed that Jordan had had affairs, perhaps a number of them, but she was stunned by how upsetting this disclosure was.

Haltingly, she asked, "Do you think I'm not—pretty enough?"

"Oh, you're pretty enough all right, but I can't see

you enjoying being fussed over and fawned over and having to worry about your makeup twenty-four hours a day." Jordan frowned contemplatively. "I guess what it boils down to is that I don't think you'd be comfortable with all the hoopla Yvette and Louis have planned."

Suddenly uneasy beneath his scrutiny, Darcy sat up and tucked her legs under her. Was he making comparisons between her and his old girlfriend? The very idea made her so angry she wanted to scream. In fact, her voice did rise heatedly as she asked, "Do you think I'm too staid to enjoy doing exciting new things?"

"That's not it at all! What I think is that you're an old-fashioned girl who enjoys the simpler pleasures of life. You don't impress me as the kind who'd want to rely on other people to provide you with excitement, and you'd be like a fish out of water in the modeling world. You saw how Yvette criticized your dress this morning. I don't think you'd be comfortable wearing—"

"Lots of gorgeous clothes?" Darcy finished for him. She was stung by the implication that he found her dowdy.

"Gorgeous, yes, lots of 'em, *no,*" Jordan countered shortly. "Didn't you hear Miles fantasizing about your wearing stuff that floats and clings and hints?"

As if to emphasize this observation, he ran his hand along her arm from wrist to elbow to shoulder, looping his index finger under the strap of her bathing suit, which was hanging loosely over her upper arm, and replacing the strap on her shoulder with painstaking care.

Determined to resist his blandishments, Darcy gritted her teeth and persisted doggedly, "I'd meet lots of new people."

"Hell, Darcy! You don't need to go into modeling for that. If you want to meet new people, you can meet them at the laundromat! Anyway, from what Ariel said about your disliking the limelight, I suspect you're romanticizing this whole thing."

"Mother was referring to my dislike of being hounded as the daughter of the famous St. Denises. It would be another matter if I were a celebrity in my own right. And if I am romanticizing modeling, who are you to criticize me for it? You're guilty of romanticizing things, too. Look at the way you talk about sailing! You told me about getting in touch with yourself and feeling in time with nature. You talked about lazy sunlit days and moonlight over tropical seas and exotic ports of call, but you didn't say a single word about sunburn or insects or seasickness or loneliness!"

"I know I didn't mention the disadvantages of life at sea," Jordan responded with maddening patience. "It goes without saying that I've had to cope with plenty of them at one time or another. But I am aware they exist, and I try to keep them in their proper perspective."

"And you think my perspective isn't proper?"

"Yes, I do think that. Not ten minutes ago you were talking about how you need to feel committed, and judging by that, I'd say your perspective is probably the only thing about you that *isn't* proper. Whether you like it or not, Goldilocks, you are a very proper young woman."

Darcy glared at him, but before she could defend herself against this charge, Jordan continued.

"Before you get all bent out of shape, I want to assure you that I mean that in the nicest possible way. You're fun to be with and bright and considerate, but most of all, you're your own person—"

"Terrific!" Darcy cut in explosively. "With that and fifty cents, I can get a cup of coffee!"

"The point is, are you willing to exchange all that for the dubious honor of becoming a nationwide symbol?"

"If I do agree to take the job, it wouldn't mean I'd have to stop being myself. I'd be selling my time and services, not my soul."

"All right," he conceded. "I may have put it too strongly, but I'm afraid right now you're attracted by the novelty of the project. When you get involved, you're likely to find out it's damned hard work."

"I don't mind hard work."

Jordan studied her with narrowed eyes. "What is it you're saying, Darcy? Do you *want* to become Perrigo's Champagne Blonde? Do you want to see yourself on billboards and TV? Is that it?"

"I haven't said that. It's just that I don't think I should dismiss this opportunity too lightly. Maybe I'll always regret it if I don't do it. Maybe I'd find out I liked being a model—and even if it turned out that I didn't like it, it's not a life sentence."

By now Darcy's agitation made it impossible for her to sit still. She jumped up and all but ran to the transom, where she leaned against the lifeline and looked absently toward the beach as she fought to regain her composure. When she felt a bit calmer, she blurted out the first thing that popped into her mind.

"Ariel says that as she gets older, she regrets the things she didn't do more than the things she did. She says that no experience is ever wasted—"

"It's you we're talking about, not your mother," Jordan pointed out brusquely.

"Well, she's known me a lot longer than you have, and apparently she thinks I'd be just right for the job. And besides, there seems to be a vast disparity between what a person wants and what she gets."

"That's defeatist talk!" Getting to his feet, Jordan came to the railing and wrapped his arms about her waist from behind. "I don't know why I'm wasting my breath trying to talk sense to you, but there's one thing I do know. I know you want me as much as I want you."

Had she been so transparent, then? Had Jordan known all along that she was jealous of the model he'd dated? Had he known that her arguments were a hastily erected, woefully inadequate defense against her longing for him?

Appalled that he should have seen through her, Darcy tried to turn away from him, but he responded by pulling her closer. He nuzzled the side of her neck and her whole body tingled with delicious sensations.

"Why fight it?" Jordan asked softly. "If you're honest

with yourself about your physical desires, maybe that will help you be honest with yourself about other areas of your life as well."

For a moment Darcy was silent. Then, easing out of his embrace, she flashed him a smile. "This excursion started out so auspiciously. It's been ages since I've felt this lighthearted and happy. Let's end it on the same note, Jordan."

He shrugged amiably. "Sure, Goldilocks, whatever you say. Shall we head back to shore then?"

"Aye, aye, skipper," she replied, wishing with all her heart that she could match his diffidence.

Chapter 7

THEY TIED UP at the anchorage Jordan had reserved for the night just before sunset, in the brief golden hour that sometimes heralded the coming of twilight in the San Juans. By mutual agreement they remained on board the *Compass Rose* to watch the flag-lowering ceremony which would soon be getting under way across the bay in Roche Harbor.

For a few minutes everything was hushed. The evening was so tranquil, so utterly still, it seemed as if time were suspended and nature holding its breath. Then the burgees and pennants and flags were lowered. The Canadian and American national anthems echoed over the water, and these were followed by "Taps." The ritual was beautifully executed, and so well timed that the last note of the bugle sounded just as the sun sank out of sight.

The puffy little clouds that floated above the treetops

were tinted dusky pink and lavender and mirrored by the glassy sea as Jordan rowed the dinghy into the marina, and a light sprinkling of stars dusted the sky as they strolled toward the house.

When they parted company, both of them heading for their rooms to change for dinner, Darcy said, "Thanks for taking me with you today, Jordan. Despite the—er, heavy conversation, I had a marvelous time."

"It was my pleasure." Jordan smiled affably and ruffled her hair. "You're a good kid, Goldilocks. We'll have to get together again soon."

He turned on his heel and bounded up the stairs two at a time, leaving a rather wistful Darcy to stare after him.

Although she was aware that his sexual attraction to her needn't signify any emotional involvement on his part, Darcy was more than a little perturbed by Jordan's nonchalance.

She also marveled at his endless store of energy. After her long walk that morning and an afternoon of sailing and swimming, she was pleasantly fatigued; so much so that she couldn't have run upstairs if her life had depended on it.

She walked along the hall to her room with dragging steps, and all the while she was changing her clothes, she had to fight the temptation to crawl into the spindle bed and go to sleep. If she hadn't been so hungry, she might have done just that.

Jordan was attentive at dinner, but Darcy knew very well that the ardent way he looked at her was part of the charade he was playing out for Ariel and Jenny's benefit. She rose to the occasion, flirting shamelessly with him and touching him at the flimsiest provocation, but she didn't talk very much. She was content to let Jordan field the questions the others asked about their afternoon together while she seemed to hang adoringly on his every word.

She told herself she was only keeping her end of their bargain, but she found that her role was distressingly easy to play. Before the meal was over, she had to acknowledge that it was no hardship at all to pretend she was falling in love with Jordan Ives.

The implications of this admission were staggering. Darcy's dessert spoon slipped out of her suddenly numb fingers, bounced off the edge of the table, and ricocheted onto the floor. As she leaned down to pick it up, her movements were jerky and uncoordinated, as if she had lost the power to control her own body, and she bumped heads with Jordan, who had also bent over to retrieve the spoon.

The corners of his eyes were crinkled with silent laughter as he reached out and ran his fingers over the reddening mark at her hairline where his stubbly jaw had grazed her skin.

"Sorry, Goldilocks," he apologized lightly. "I'll ask Olive to bring you another spoon."

"Never mind," Darcy hurriedly replied. "I'd finished anyway."

Her startling realization had taken away her appetite. The white-chocolate mousse she'd thought so delicious only a minute before no longer appealed to her, and listlessly she pushed it away.

A few short hours ago Jordan had told her he knew she was attracted to him. "Why fight it?" he'd asked, and he hadn't even known the half of it. Now she asked herself if she *could* fight her desire for him. How could she resist him when his smile, his touch, the sound of his voice, the way his eyes crinkled, were so damnably, gloriously exciting? When even the scrape of his beard against her skin was seductive?

She saw him gazing at her with his intense blue eyes and tried to return his smile. She clenched her hands in her lap to hide their trembling, but his reaction told her how wan and shaken she must look.

As if he knew what she was thinking, as if he knew what she was *feeling*, he covered both of her hands with one of his and gave them a gentle squeeze.

"Don't worry," he said softly. "It's going to be all right."

What a curious thing to say! thought Darcy. But even stranger than the reassurance he'd given her was the fact that, for the moment, she believed him!

The final revelation was postponed by Jenny's announcement that coffee and liqueurs would be served in the living room. Darcy was acutely aware of Jordan as he held her chair and escorted her away from the table. Once she was in the living room, however, she was able to keep her distance from him, and she began to regain her composure.

By the time Jordan, Louis, and Miles announced they had some business to discuss and excused themselves to go into the den, she had convinced herself that the idea of her actually falling in love with Jordan Ives was preposterous. It was simply another product of her overactive imagination. The chemistry between them was more potent than anything she'd ever experienced, so she couldn't deny that she was attracted to him physically, but that was *all*.

Apparently the way Darcy watched Jordon as the men filed out of the room was not lost upon Yvette. She ended her conversation with Harry Templeton and hurried to sit in the chair next to Darcy's.

"Quel homme!" she exclaimed lustily. "Jordan is the most divine man, is he not, Dar-cee? If I did not fear Louis's jealousy, perhaps I would give you a little competition."

"You're far too modest, Madame Perrigo," Darcy replied. "If you were interested in winning a man's attention, there'd be no competition."

"Merci, ma petite." Yvette laughed delightedly. "How refreshing it is to find that you are as diplomatic as you are beautiful."

"Many thanks—for both compliments," Darcy said. "Though after some of the comments made about my appearance this morning, beautiful doesn't seem quite the word."

"Take it from an expert, *ma petite*. Beauty is an illusion almost any woman can create. With the right makeup, the right clothes—who knows?" Yvette moved her shoulders in an eloquent Gallic gesture. "Perhaps you would be enough of a beauty to make even such a discriminating man as Jordan Ives sit up and take notice."

"Why do you say that? Do you think Jordan is overimpressed by superficial appearances?"

"What man isn't?" Yvette asked wryly. "There are those who subscribe to the theory that if Cleopatra's nose had been a few millimeters longer, the whole course of history might have been drastically altered."

"So I've heard," said Darcy, "except I heard it in connection with Helen of Troy's nose. But it doesn't really matter one way or the other. I'm not naive enough to believe that something as inconsequential as the length of a woman's nose—or the turn of her ankle, or the size of her breasts—has ever had any significant influence on the outcome of truly important events."

"Perhaps you are right, Dar-cee. And then again—perhaps you are not!" Yvette smiled impishly. "One thing is certain. Men might say it is some inner quality that gives a woman appeal. They might define it as a combination of wit, compassion, and a capacity for love. They might even believe it, and in a long-term relationship they would discover it's true. But if you show me a woman who claims her appearance isn't important to her man, I'll show you a fraud or a fool! Before one can inspire devotion, one must capture and hold the interest, and most men cannot resist the bait of a bewitching wrapping."

"And have you some special reason for believing this is any more true of Jordan than of other men?"

"But of course!" Yvette glanced at the others as if to

calculate the chances of anyone overhearing them. When she saw that Ariel, Jenny, and Harry were on the far side of the room, absorbed in their own conversation as they arranged the cards and score pads on the bridge table, she inquired in lowered tones, "Do you not know about Sunny Gardiner?"

"Sunny Gardiner?" Darcy knitted her brows, trying to recall where she had heard the name before, and when she did remember, her heart sank. "Isn't she a model?"

"That's right. What's more, she is one of the very best."

Praying that Yvette's answer would not be the one she anticipated, Darcy asked, "What does she have to do with Jordan?"

"She used to be his fiancée." Yvette leaned closer. Her voice was barely audible as she continued, "And, Dar-cee, if you could see Sunny, you would know how much Jordan prizes beauty in a woman. Her eyes are as green as forest pools. Her skin is like rich cream. If only her hair were fair instead of dark, we would not have had to search far and wide for our Champagne Blonde! Sunny is the very essence of feminine perfection. And she possesses not only great beauty, but chic! And glamour! And such a figure! Sunny is..." Unable to find superlatives grand enough to encompass Sunny Gardiner's charms, Yvette sketched an alluring female figure in the air with her hands.

When Darcy responded with a skeptical shake of her head, Yvette rolled her eyes soulfully and lamented, "Ah, Dar-cee, I can see you think I am exaggerating, but it is the truth nevertheless. And Jordan—how he adored Sunny. How he worshipped her! He was mad about her—"

"She sounds like a paragon," Darcy interjected coolly. "But if Jordan cared that deeply for Sunny, why didn't he marry her?"

"He had no choice, Dar-cee. You see, it was Sunny who ended their affair."

Darcy found it difficult to believe that any woman would pass up the chance to marry Jordan. "Do you mean Sunny jilted him?" she asked incredulously.

"I hesitate to put it so strongly," Yvette replied. "To say Sunny jilted him implies a degree of betrayal, and neither of them was guilty of infidelity. To this day they are dear, dear friends. They have a great *tendresse* for one another."

"Then what happened to break them up?"

"It was simply that both of them were so busy with their careers. Sunny's work required that she travel, while Jordan had to remain in Bellingham. Until about three years ago his finances were precarious. He was holding on to his grandfather's business by the skin of his teeth, and he rarely left the boatyard.

"At the same time, Sunny had become more and more in demand. In the end they had so little time together, I suppose it was inevitable that they would drift apart, but it was a great tragedy. They were glorious together—so well suited."

A huge lump had gathered in Darcy's throat. She swallowed hard, attempting to dislodge it, but her voice was husky when she said, "I know why you're telling me this, Madame Perrigo."

An appreciative gurgle of laughter escaped Yvette. "Of course you do! I expected you would without my having to spell it out. After all, as Ariel has so often pointed out, you are her daughter."

Darcy smiled ruefully. "When you first came over and sat beside me, I was going to ask why you hadn't gone off to talk business with the men. I mean, it's apparent that you're as involved with running Perrigo Wines as your husband. Now I see you had business of your own to conduct."

"Louis and Miles are trying to come to terms with Jordan over the use of his sailboat for one of our TV commercials," Yvette said crisply. "Picking nits regarding lease provisions is not my forte."

"Your forte is perhaps making people offers they can't refuse?"

"If you wish to put it so bluntly," Yvette agreed equably. "I certainly hope *you* won't refuse, Dar-cee." Her eyes sparkled with deviltry as she inquired, "Have you been too wrapped up in Jordan to think of anything else, or have you given some consideration to our proposal?"

"I've thought about it," Darcy replied gravely, "and I didn't really need the object lesson about Sunny Gardiner to realize how much Jordan prefers the unique to the humdrum. The way he talks about sailing makes that fairly clear."

"Naturally it does to one as perceptive as you. But in order to appreciate how deeply ingrained his taste for the exotic is, you must understand that Jordan was deprived of the usual pleasures of youth. His parents were killed in a plane crash when he was seventeen, and his grandfather died less than six months later. Jasper Ives was a fine man. In some ways he was a near genius, or so I've been led to believe. He earned the unwavering loyalty of both his employees and his customers, but he was highly impractical. One might even say that he was an *idiot savant,* because he had no head for business at all."

Yvette shook her head disparagingly. Her tone was tinged with contempt as she went on: "In his later years Jasper even lost the rights to manufacture several devices of his own invention. I gather they were crucial to the survival of the firm, and as a consequence he had to borrow to the limit of his credit line. At the time of his death the boatyard was near bankruptcy."

"Jordan told me a little about his grandfather today," Darcy said softly. "He admired him greatly."

"Yes, he did," Yvette affirmed. "In fact, when Jordan took over the reins, he was advised to unload the business, but his admiration for his grandfather prompted him to accomplish the impossible by salvaging what he could. And he wasn't satisfied merely to put the boatyard back in the black and keep it in the family. It seems

Jasper made certain innovations in boat design and in self-steering apparatus, and Jordan was determined that someday his grandfather should receive the recognition he deserved."

"That's quite an ambitious undertaking for anyone, let alone a teenager," said Darcy.

"But that wasn't all, Dar-cee. Jordan was saddled with the responsibility for his aunt's welfare as well. While Jenny is a darling, when it comes to business matters, she has inherited all of Jasper's failings and none of his virtues. She is about as practical as a two-year-old. So at an age when most young men are indulging in youthful escapades, concerned about nothing more serious than whether Papa will permit them to use the family car on Saturday night, Jordan had to keep his nose to the grindstone."

"Are you saying that Jordan is going through some sort of delayed adolescence?" asked Darcy.

"No, nothing as unkind as that," Yvette hastily replied. "What I'm saying is, now that the boatyard is secure and Jenny's holdings are well in hand and Jordan himself is financially independent, it is not surprising that he should want to do some of the things he could only dream about through all those years of hard work."

For a while Yvette was silent, allowing Darcy to assimilate this new information about Jordan. Her patience was rewarded when Darcy said rather cautiously, "Madame Perrigo, if I agree to do the modeling for your advertising campaign, what would be involved?"

"The first step would be to get some pictures made of you," Yvette explained. "You understand we cannot commit ourselves until we have seen how well you photograph."

Darcy nodded.

"If you're as photogenic as I suspect you are, we would ask you to sign an exclusive contract with us— perhaps for six months. This would allow us to film the commercials and prepare several print ads for market testing. After we've launched the campaign, we would exercise our option on your services for a longer period of time.

"We've planned quite an extravanganza for the debut of our Champagne Blonde," Yvette continued, warming to her topic. "The publicity releases are to coincide with the annual wine-judging gala at San Francisco's Palace of Fine Arts, and the masterstroke is that we've an excellent chance of being awarded a gold medal for our chenin blanc. Then there would be talk shows. Louis and I would handle those, but we would expect you to put in an appearance.

"As to specifics, I've yet to hear any of our models complain about her fee. I'm sure we can agree on terms that would be satisfactory to all of us."

"What kind of ads are you planning?" When the older woman glanced at her quizzically, Darcy stammered, "I—I wouldn't want to look silly—"

"We wouldn't want you to look silly either, *ma petite!*" Yvette exclaimed. "We hope our campaign will have a certain snob appeal, so rest assured, it's not a 'jiggle show' we're casting! Yes, we want to emphasize your looks and sex appeal, but only up to a point, and always with good taste!"

"I'd have to decide what to do about my job—"

"I can appreciate that you'll want to give your employer some notice," Yvette sympathized. "Your mother tells me you enjoy your work immensely, but if you sign with us, you'll have to give it up—at least temporarily. Perhaps you could arrange to take a leave of absence."

"Perhaps," Darcy echoed noncommittally. Yvette's explanation had raised as many questions as it had answered, and she felt more confused than ever. "You realize I've never done any modeling."

"Since we decided a totally new face would be best for our campaign, we had expected the model we chose to be inexperienced. I can only guess at your misgivings,

Dar-cee, but I know how bewildering this must be for
you. I promise you I will work very closely with you
until you're ready to go it alone. I think you would learn
very quickly."

Still uncertain, Darcy chose to stall for time. "Can I
give you my answer tomorrow?" she asked. "I'd like to
talk this over with my mother before I come to a decision."

"But of course! Tomorrow will be fine."

Yvette rose, indicating that the interview was over,
but before she left, she paused to study Darcy's face in
the lamplight.

"You know, *ma petite,*" she said, "once you were
established as our symbol, you could branch out if you
wished. You'd be free to work for other clients as long
as there was no conflict of interests. With my help and
promotion and your assets, it's possible that the sky will
be your limit. If your look catches on, your future could
be whatever you choose to make it."

On that note Yvette went off to join the bridge players,
and after she'd arranged to meet with Ariel when they'd
finished the first rubber, Darcy was left to her own devices.

She prowled about the house aimlessly, wondering
how long Jordan's business conference was likely to continue. Her wandering carried her to her bedroom, and
when she saw the selection of books and periodicals on
the bookshelf, she curled up on the windowseat with a
recent copy of *Vogue*.

She was preoccupied. Her mind raced with thoughts
of her conversation with Yvette, and she thumbed through
the magazine abstractedly until she came across a per-
fume ad that featured Sunny Gardiner.

Suddenly alert, she studied the picture of the raven-
haired model for so long a time that when she closed her
eyes she could still see the picture.

Yvette hadn't been exaggerating. Sunny's coloring

was striking, her features classic, and her figure every bit as alluring as the one Yvette had outlined. She was Scarlett O'Hara in the flesh.

Darcy closed the magazine, set it aside, and returned to the living room for her talk with Ariel. Within half an hour she was back in the tower room, preparing to go to bed.

She felt oddly dejected, and she glanced toward the rose Jordan had given her, thinking it might lift her spirits. But the rose had withered. Most of the petals had faded and dropped off the bud, and she was left with only the memory of its beauty. And that, too, would fade with time.

This thought made her eyes sting with tears. Somehow it seemed appropriate that the rose hadn't survived the weekend after all.

Chapter 8

JORDAN WOKE DARCY early the next morning, pounding at her door until he'd roused her from a deep sleep. She was barely conscious when she dragged herself out of bed and pulled a dressing gown around her shoulders, and she was speechless with surprise when she peered through the partially open door and saw who was causing the disturbance.

Feigning innocence, Jordan asked, "Did I wake you?"

"You probably woke the whole house," Darcy replied irritably. "Is something wrong?"

"Nope. I just thought you might want to go fishing with me."

"Are the fish awake this early?"

Unscathed by her sarcasm, Jordan grinned and pushed against the door with one hand, opening it wider. His eyes trailed over her, assessing her from head to toe, taking in her tousled hair and bare feet, lingering on the soft rise and fall of her breasts beneath the filmy bodice of her nightgown. When she folded her robe more snugly about herself, he chuckled.

"You know, Goldilocks, you're kinda cute first thing in the morning."

"So are you," she responded sourly. This morning he was wearing utilitarian gray jogging pants with a matching sweat shirt, and he was more devastatingly attractive than any one man had a right to be.

"How about it?" he inquired lazily.

She stared at him uncomprehendingly, but her reserve began to thaw under the warmth of his smile.

"How about what?" she asked.

"Going fishing." He passed one hand in front of her face as if to test her vision. "Is your memory failing, or aren't you awake yet?"

"Oh, I'm awake all right, and as long as I am, I may as well go fishing with you. There's nothing else to do at this ungodly hour."

Once again Jordan's eyes strayed over her, and this time they settled on the tender curve of her mouth. Bending close to her, he drawled, "I can think of a few things I'd rather do. If you'd invite me in, I'd be happy to tell you about them. I might even be persuaded to give you a demonstration."

"That won't be necessary," Darcy countered brightly, more tempted by his spur-of-the-moment pass than she cared to admit. "I already know what they are."

"And?"

"And I think we'd better go fishing."

"Okay," Jordan agreed cheerfully. "Meet you outside in ten minutes."

"Ten minutes," she murmured as Jordan strode away from her down the hall.

She wasted two minutes of the allotted time questioning her eager acceptance of his invitation. She didn't like fishing very much, and while she considered herself an early riser, in her estimation five o'clock didn't qualify as morning. The sun wasn't even up yet.

It was not until the deep rumble of Jordan's voice, followed by the softer twang of Olive Hyatt's, came through the open bedroom window that Darcy was shaken out of her stupor.

She dashed into the bathroom to brush her teeth and wash the sleep from her eyes, and she dressed in record time, pulling on underwear, a pair of shorts, a long-sleeved cotton blouse, and sneakers. She ran a comb through her hair and tied it back with a scarf. Then, grabbing up her sun hat, her beach bag, and tanning cream, she hurried to join Jordan.

Just as Darcy stepped through the front door, Olive appeared from the kitchen wing of the house carrying a picnic basket. As she handed the basket to Jordan, the housekeeper remarked, "It's only coffee, orange juice, and croissants, but I packed enough to see you through till breakfast."

"Olive, my darlin'," said Jordan, "my stomach is deeply indebted to you." Sweeping the housekeeper into his arms, he gave her an enormous bear hug.

"That's enough of your blarney," Olive scolded. She was trying to scowl as she pulled away from Jordan and tugged at her apron to straighten it, but her face was flushed with pleasure. "If you want to show your gratitude, try bringing me back some fish!"

"Will do." Laughing, Jordan collected the poles and tackle box and started down the drive.

"Usually all he comes home with is a tall tale about the one that got away," Olive explained to Darcy, who was already scurrying to catch up with Jordan and so had no chance to reply.

Once they were out on the water, however, it didn't take her long to figure out why Jordan habitually came home from a fishing expedition empty-handed. For all his rush to be on his way, he did very little fishing. He cast both lines, then ignored them while they drifted with the current in the middle of the bay, letting the outgoing tide take the dinghy and the lines where it would.

When it became apparent that Jordan had no intention of paying any further attention to the poles, Darcy asked, "Why do you bother bringing the fishing gear?"

"It's my way of gambling," Jordan answered. "Sometimes I actually snag something."

"But mostly you just like being on the water."

"Yep," Jordan agreed laconically. Waving one arm in a broad gesture that took in the wide expanse of water that separated them from the tree-lined shore, he said, "It's freer out here. A man feels less hemmed in."

Darcy wondered why Jordan's admission that he disliked being constrained should cause a strange sinking sensation in her stomach. Then she decided she must be hungry. She opened the hamper, found a roll for each of them, and poured out some juice. As she handed Jordan his coffee, she reminded him, "You promised Olive you'd bring home some fish today."

"There's always a gang of kids fishing off the docks. I'll buy something from one of them."

Darcy took a bite of her croissant and chewed in thoughtful silence.

"Olive is very fond of you," she observed.

"I'm fond of her, too," said Jordan. "She used to run my grandfather's house, so we go back a long way. My parents traveled quite a lot when I was a boy, and I used to see more of Olive than I did of my mother."

Jordan helped himself to another croissant and offered one to Darcy, and for a time neither of them spoke. Instead, they concentrated on the contents of their picnic basket. Both of them ate hungrily while the sun moved higher in the sky, finally climbing above the treetops to throw a hazy golden mantle over the water.

Now that it was almost seven thirty, the harbor was waking up. People appeared on the decks of some of the boats, flags were raised, sails were hoisted, an outboard engine coughed and sprang to life.

Jordan stretched contentedly and peeled off his shirt, and Darcy tied on her hat and rummaged through her beach bag for her suntan lotion. Jordan watched with more interest than the activity warranted as she smoothed on the cream. When she had finished, he reached out and tweaked her nose.

"Did you know you're getting freckles?" he teased.

Disconcerted, Darcy looked away from him. She crumbled the last of her croissant and tossed the crumbs to some ducks that were swimming nearby, hunting for their own breakfasts.

After cushioning the prow of the boat with his shirt, Jordan lay back with his arms folded behind his head. He studied the birds as they squawked and scrambled after the bread crumbs.

"Why are you embarrassed about having freckles?" he mused aloud. "They're cute. It's for sure you look better now than you did yesterday morning. You're less washed out." Turning his gaze upon her, he asked, "What kind of work do you do that keeps you indoors all day?"

Rankled by his penchant for paying her left-handed compliments and even more upset that it should matter so much to her whether he thought she was pretty, Darcy replied shortly, "I'm a librarian."

"Hey, no kidding! You're really a librarian?"

Darcy sighed. "Yes," she said, "I really am."

"But you're not at all—"

"Bookish?" she supplied. "Surely you haven't succumbed to the myth that all librarians are dried up spinsters whose only experience of life is obtained vicariously, through reading?"

"I guess I have to plead guilty to that charge," said Jordan sheepishly.

"Well let me assure you, librarians come in all shapes and sizes and personality types—"

"I'm sure they do, Goldilocks."

"I've known quite a few librarians," she went on as if he'd disagreed with her, "and so far there hasn't been a shy and retiring one among 'em."

"You're living proof of that," said Jordan. He smiled at her, and Darcy's irritation evaporated, melting beneath the warmth in his eyes.

"I'm sorry," she said weakly. "In case you haven't noticed, at times I'm inclined to overreact."

"Oh, I've noticed," Jordan replied. "I've also noticed that you sometimes over*act,* but in this case I can't say I blame you. Would you tell me about your work?"

"I wouldn't want to bore you," she demured. "Tim used to fall asleep the minute I'd start talking about the library."

"I thought we'd established that I'm not Tim Cummins," Jordan said curtly. "Are you interested in your work, or are you just putting in time?"

"Well of course *I* think it's interesting, and since I'm a children's librarian, my job provides an outlet for my— er, tendency to dramatize things."

"So tell me about it," he insisted, and when she did, she found that he was unexpectedly attentive.

She began by telling him about her supervisor, Mr. Pritchard, who seemed to labor under the misconception that the primary duty of a librarian was to protect the books from the people who came into the library. But Jordan was such a good listener that she went on from there, telling him enthusiastically about some of the children who were regulars at her story hour for preschoolers.

She told him about Ricky, the all-American five-year-old who brought her caterpillars and bubblegum and bunches of wildflowers. She told him about four-year-old Alison, who swore she was going to be a nurse, a fireman, *and* a ballerina when she grew up, and about Jackie Mori, who at the tender age of three had taught himself to read.

It was only when the Sunday morning stillness was broken by the steeple bells from the chapel that she realized how long she had been talking.

"I don't know what's gotten into me," she hastily apologized. "I'm not usually a marathon talker."

"Hey, it's okay!" Jordan assured her. He sat up, pulled on his sweat shirt, and began reeling in the fishing lines. "The only thing is, since it's obvious how much you like working with children, I'm even more puzzled as to why you'd have to think twice about turning down the modeling job with the Perrigos."

"Normally, I wouldn't."

"Then why should you now? Unless . . . is it the money?"

"Partly." Sighing, Darcy confided, "I'm concerned about my mother. I'm afraid she's having financial problems."

"Have you had a chance to talk to her yet?"

"Yes, for all the good it did. I finally managed to corner her last night, but I don't know any more now than I did before our talk."

"What did she say?"

"To begin with, she gave me a song and dance about why she got me to come here this weekend."

"The old runaround," Jordan said knowingly.

"And then some," Darcy confirmed. "She told me a story about how stubborn I was when I was a little girl. It had something to do with my entering a phase when I'd only eat what I could scrounge up for myself. She said she resorted to hiding my meals where I'd come across them in the cupboards—"

"And in all the years since then, you haven't outgrown that phase," Jordan completed the narrative. "The moral being that in the banquet of life, she's still forced to lay things out for you, then stand by helplessly, hoping you'll discover for yourself that Mother knows best."

"You got it!" Darcy exclaimed, astonished by the accuracy of his interpretation. "But how in the world did you know? Those were her words, almost precisely!"

"My aunt has used the same story on me a time or two." After a single unperturbed glance at the empty hooks on the fishing lines, Jordan propped the poles in the bow of the dinghy and began rowing toward shore. "Did Ariel actually say she needed your help to make ends meet?"

"She's too proud to come right out with a thing like that, but she admitted that inflation's been depleting her capital, and she's feeling the same economic pinch as everyone else. Then, too, there's her house here. I don't believe she really wants to sell it. She's also wearing some of last year's clothes—"

"That's not like the Ariel I know," Jordan admitted.

"No, it isn't like her at all. And there's one more thing. The other night, when she phoned me from L.A., she talked about how expensive the call was going to be. At the time I didn't think too much about it, but it's highly atypical for my mother to complain about long-distance rates. She's accustomed to phoning halfway around the world at the drop of a hat."

"You said your worries about Ariel are only part of the reason you haven't turned down Louis and Yvette's offer," Jordan probed.

Darcy widened her eyes at him, praying for inspiration. She should have known the instant she'd made this slip that he would return to it.

"Did I?" she stalled, hoping she sounded ingenuous.

"Yes, you did."

She could hardly tell Jordan that she was willing to try almost anything short of a felony that might make him take her more seriously. She couldn't tell him that she wanted him to see her as something more than "a cute kid" and "a good sport." But with him eyeing her so dubiously, she found it impossible to dissemble. She was left with no alternative but to tell a half truth.

Setting her chin firmly, she offered the excuse, "The rest of it is personal. I'd rather not go into it just now."

"Very well," Jordan said coolly. "But you sound as

if you've already made up your mind to go ahead with it."

Darcy inhaled deeply. Matching him for coolness, she replied, "As a matter of fact, I have."

She watched him circumspectly, trying to read his expression, but his face was impassive. His vocal response, on the other hand, displayed a frank skepticism.

"Well, Goldilocks, it's your funeral," he said lightly.

"I don't expect you to approve," Darcy protested, "but you needn't be so discouraging!"

"Can I help it if I think you're making a big mistake?" Jordan returned sharply. "I saw your reaction to the way the others carried on at lunch yesterday. You didn't much care for being treated like a commodity. I don't think you should jump into this thing until you know exactly what you want."

"For someone who doesn't believe in giving advice, you're very quick to hand it out!"

Jordan frowned at this accusation. "I'm not advising you, Darcy," he declared. "I'm simply stating my opinion."

After this exchange it seemed to Darcy there was nothing more to be said. She took refuge in petulant silence, but if Jordan noticed her withdrawal, it didn't dampen his spirits.

He was whistling as he beached the dinghy, and he laughed and joked with the group of boys on the pier while he struck a bargain for some of their fish. He paused to wrap the fish and put it in the picnic basket and was whistling again as he led the way back to the house.

Since he was pointedly ignoring her ill humor, she was totally unprepared for his change of attitude when, on arriving at their destination, Jordan suddenly dropped the fishing gear and the basket on the front steps and turned to her. Looping his arms about her shoulders, he drew her close and buried his face in the curve of her neck.

"Don't look now," he cautioned, "but we have an audience. Ariel and Jenny are watching us from the living room window."

Darcy tried to crane her neck so that she could see the window over his shoulder, but he stopped her, framing her face between his hands.

"I said *don't look,*" he muttered.

His tightening hold on her underscored the command, and his mouth came down on hers, silencing her objections with a feather-light kiss, asking her to capitulate with the sweet play of his tongue as he traced the curve of her upper lip. And when she sighed her surrender, opening her mouth and melting into his arms, his hands reinforced the gentle demands his lips were making, tugging her hat off and tossing it aside, smoothing her hair away from her face, sliding insistently around the nape of her neck, moving restlessly over her back to mold her closer to the proud, hard length of his body.

It's only a kiss, Darcy told herself. But she was drowning in the wake of undiluted passion. By the time Jordan's mouth released hers, she couldn't think clearly. She was weak with longing, aching with need for him.

It was not until later that day, when she had boarded the ferry and was on her way back to Anacortes, that Darcy acknowledged how profoundly Jordan affected her.

Before she'd left Roche Harbor, she had thrown caution to the wind and agreed to accept the modeling assignment as Perrigo's Champagne Blonde.

Lunch had been festive. The wine had flowed like water, and when Louis had toasted the campaign, this time she'd drunk the toast.

Jenny cried, "Congratulations, Darcy!"

"It's Yvette and Louis you should congratulate, Jenny," Harry Templeton contradicted, his eyes twinkling. "This lovely young lady will sell entire shiploads of champagne for them, and the most they'll have to do is endorse the checks and fill out the deposit slips when it's time to bank the profits."

"I don't know if it'll be that easy," Miles laughed, "but I'm positive of one thing. Darcy is perfect for the job. Absolutely perfect!"

Yvette interrupted her list of instructions to say, "You won't be sorry, Dar-cee. As I told you last night, your future is secured. It can be whatever you want it to be."

"Darling," Ariel applauded, hugging her warmly, "I can't tell you how thrilled I am. I know you'll be fabulous."

After lunch, Jordan went with Darcy to the ferry to see her off, and she'd used this time alone with him to try to justify her decision. He'd been less than enthusiastic, but he'd said only, "I hope you won't regret it, Goldilocks. If it's what you really want, I don't suppose you will."

He'd kissed her lightly and walked away, leaving her standing numbly by the railing while the ferry slid away from the landing, waving to him, already missing him.

At the last minute Jordan cupped his hands to his mouth and shouted, "See you in Seattle!"

His voice was barely audible above the loud chug of the engines, but her heart leaped with anticipation. Even after Jordan had left the landing, Darcy remained on deck. She watched the harbor recede until the island had become a tiny speck in the distance and her mind began to function.

She fervently hoped Jordan had forgotten how coolly she'd received his suggestion that they continue to date beyond the weekend. She hoped that he would make good his promise to see her in Seattle.

She had known all along that she had no desire to be a celebrity, and she didn't give a damn about becoming Perrigos' Champagne Blonde.

It was Jordan she wanted. She was stunned by the realization that although he might be playing a game of make-believe, she was playing for keeps.

She was falling in love with him.

Chapter 9

THE NEXT FEW weeks were the most hectic Darcy had ever known. On Monday she gave notice to Mr. Pritchard, and perhaps to get even with her for her defection, he scheduled her for more than her share of extra hours filling in for vacationing employees.

Her initial session with Jere Winston went very well, in all likelihood because she didn't know enough to be nervous when she reported to his studio for her test shots. The rapier-thin, hypertense photographer chain-smoked and talked constantly. All during the shoot, he bombarded her with directions, shouting to make himself heard above the raucous blare of rock music on his tape deck.

"Raise your left shoulder," he ordered, "Lift your chin. A little less smile, sweetie. Talk to me with your eyes. Let me have more energy!"

The lights were unbelievably hot, the huge fans that

were supposed to simulate gentle breezes blowing through her hair produced gale-force winds, and her ears rang from Jere Winston's booming voice. All in all, posing for the photographer was unlike anything Darcy had ever experienced.

On the day his photographs were delivered, she met with Yvette Perrigo for what she assumed was going to be a leisurely dinner, but as soon as she walked into Yvette's hotel suite, she was caught up in a whirlwind of preparations for the advertising campaign.

Yvette proclaimed that the pictures were superb. "The camera loves you, Dar-cee, which is half the battle, but we have our work cut out for us if you are to be ready to begin the print ads and the commercial next month. First of all, I'd like the photos to show a bit more of your lovely bone structure. We can do a certain amount with makeup, but I've made out a diet for you. I want you to lose at least five pounds. Eight would be better, and ten best of all. Secondly, I want you to work on your suntan—"

Yvette's list of dos and don'ts seemed endless. It went on interminably throughout the meeting. When room service delivered dinner, there was *coq au vin* for Yvette and a low-calorie salad for Darcy. Yvette continued her lecture, pausing only to take an occasional mouthful of her chicken. She ate very slowly, but somehow she managed to consume all of it while Darcy picked halfheartedly at the weight-watcher's special and envied every mouthwatering bite the other woman took.

When Darcy said good night and left for her apartment, her head was crammed with instructions, but her stomach was woefully empty.

That evening proved to Darcy that Yvette had not misrepresented her intentions when she'd claimed she planned to work very closely with the model who was selected for the Champagne Blonde campaign. Over the next few days Yvette spent so much time with her that

Darcy began to feel as if she'd acquired a living shadow.

When she wasn't at the library working, it was Yvette who supervised her activities. She rushed from wardrobe fittings to the aerobic dance class in which Yvette had enrolled her to the crash course in modeling that was also administered by Yvette. The trampoline, the treadmill, and the other exercise equipment that Yvette had had delivered to her apartment threatened to crowd her out of her living room.

Yvette requested and suggested. She prodded, implored, and dictated. If all else failed, she was not above nagging, but in one way or another, she made it plain that for the duration of their business association, the most minute details of Darcy's life were subject to her approval.

If this hadn't already been apparent, the following weekend would have clarified the point. Jordan sailed the *Compass Rose* into Seattle on Saturday, and Darcy and he spent most of the weekend painting the dinghy. But first, the hull had to be scraped and sanded.

Jordan told Darcy she shouldn't help with that particular chore. When he saw how eagerly she attacked the job, he warned her what Yvette's reaction would be.

"It isn't that I don't appreciate your willingness to help," he said, "but Yvette's going to hit the ceiling when she finds out what you've been up to."

"How will she know?" asked Darcy. "I don't have to tell her."

"Take a look at your hands," Jordan said dryly.

Darcy did as he suggested, and she saw that there was no way she could keep Yvette from learning what she'd done over the weekend. Her fingernails were jagged and quite a lot shorter than they'd been before she'd started sanding the boat. Several of them were broken almost to the quick. Not only that, but her hands were roughened from working with the sandpaper and stained by the pigments from the old paint.

"Oh, well," she said negligently. "It's too late now." Besides, she added silently, she refused to give up a single moment of this weekend with Jordan.

At times they talked about serious things as they worked. At others, especially toward the end of the day, when both of them were slaphappy with weariness, they got a little silly and most anything would send them into gales of laughter. And sometimes they were contentedly, companionably silent.

Long before the job was done, Darcy had discovered that painting the dinghy was *fun*. In fact, because Jordan and she were working together, that backbreaking job turned out to be more fun than she'd had in ages. She was sorry when they were finished and even sorrier when Sunday evening rolled around.

Jordan grilled some salmon steaks for dinner that night and they ate on board the *Compass Rose*. It was after ten by the time they started the drive across town to her apartment, and Darcy had to struggle to stay awake. During the drive she fell asleep, and when Jordan parked the car at her apartment complex and kissed her awake, she thought at first that she must be dreaming. Then she realized he really was kissing her, and she responded hungrily to the sweet pressure of his lips against her own.

"Mmmm," she murmured drowsily, snuggling her cheek against his shoulder. "What a delicious way to wake up."

"Careful, Goldilocks. If you give me any encouragement at all, I'll be sorely tempted to take advantage of your semiconscious state." Folding her closer in his arms, Jordan buried his face in her hair and whispered, "You're very sweet when you're sleeping."

"You're very sweet when I'm sleeping, too," Darcy returned, surprising herself with her sauciness.

Jordan laughed and walked her to her door. He bade her a husky good night and promised he'd sail down from Bellingham to see her the next weekend, but he didn't ask to come in. He had to phone for a taxi to get back to the marina, but he said he wanted to walk part of the way, and Darcy realized that he really didn't intend to take advantage of her.

Later, when she was alone in her room, she had trouble falling asleep. Her bed seemed so big and wide and *empty*. She tried to convince herself that she was grateful Jordan hadn't renewed his invitation to share her bed, but she longed for his arms around her and wished that he had stayed.

The new week began as Jordan had predicted it would. Yvette did hit the ceiling when she saw the condition of Darcy's hands, but once she had given Darcy a lecture on the importance of beautifully kept Champagne Blonde hands, things settled into a routine of sorts.

Darcy began her days half an hour earlier so that she could jog on the treadmill before it was time to report to the library. She sleepwalked through her hours at work, then passed the rest of the day trying valiantly to keep up with the rigorous pace Yvette set for her. She was exhausted when she fell into bed at night, but the days flew by. She considered this a definite plus, because she was marking time until Jordan's return.

Another Saturday arrived, and with it Jordan, but this weekend was less satisfactory than the previous one. Perhaps by now Darcy cared too much for Jordan. She was frightened by the intensity of her feelings. Maybe she lacked self-confidence, or maybe Jordan was too sure of himself. After the way Tim had used her, perhaps she was too wary to ever really trust Jordan completely.

All Darcy knew for certain was that she was afraid of being hurt. She was also tired and hungry most of the time, and short-tempered *all* of the time. She didn't know if she could bear saying good night to Jordan at her front door, and she dreaded saying good-bye to him on Sunday evening. But when the weekend was over, she had managed to do both of these things.

"Try to get more sleep," Jordan advised her coolly. "That might sweeten your disposition." He kissed her on the forehead and left her, saying noncommittally, "I'll be in touch."

Darcy watched after him as he walked toward the elevator, wishing he'd given her a real kiss—a lover's kiss. And when the elevator doors had closed behind him, she felt hollow and incomplete. She felt a terrible sense of loss, and she swore that if only Jordan would give her another chance, if only he would come to see her next weekend, she would not say good night to him at the front door again.

Darcy received her retainer from the Perrigos the following Thursday. She wrote out a check to her mother that same evening, and she mailed it to Ariel with a deep sense of accomplishment. But as the next week progressed, a new problem developed.

Now Darcy found that she hadn't a moment to call her own. She had grown resigned to the long hours and the hunger pangs. She'd gotten used to the drudgery and the aching muscles and the medicinal smell of liniment, but she missed having a quiet time eacy day. She missed her privacy. Most of all, she missed Jordan.

He hadn't come to Seattle the previous Saturday, and he hadn't called or written. Although he'd said he'd be in touch, he hadn't specified when that might be, and she was very much afraid he'd given her a not-too-subtle brush-off.

Nevertheless, no matter how tired she was, she rushed to answer the telephone whenever it rang. When ten days had gone by and she still hadn't heard from him, she placed a call to his boatyard and was told he was not there. She tried again the next day.

This time the switchboard operator informed her, "Mr. Ives won't be available until the weekend. But if it's an emergency, you can contact him by ship-to-shore."

When Darcy replied that there was nothing urgent about her call, the operator offered to relay any message, but Darcy told her there was none and hung up.

The only message, she thought glumly, was the one

she'd just received. In the contest for Jordan's affections, the *Compass Rose* was the hands-down winner. Darcy Cummins was merely an also-ran.

Darcy arrived at the Perrigos' hotel suite that Friday evening to find that Louis was waiting for her.

"Yvette was unexpectedly called out, so I offered to fill in for her," he explained. "I wanted to talk to you about next week's schedule anyway, and perhaps it's all to the good." He sat her down beside him on the sofa and studied her soberly. "You're looking a bit peaked, Darcy. Has my wife been overdoing it?"

"No, I wouldn't say that." Darcy smiled shakily. "Madame Perrigo has been strict with me, but since the time is so limited, I realize that's necessary."

"Something is troubling you," Louis persisted. "Won't you tell me what it is? Perhaps I could be of help."

"Well," she replied hesitantly, "this was my last day at the library—"

"I see," said Louis. "Now that the bridge is burning behind you, you're afraid you've been imprudent. You're wondering whether you've done the right thing."

"Yes, I am, but not for the reason you're thinking. It's just that, at the lunch hour today some of the people I worked with threw a going-away party for me. Everyone was saying we'd see each other often—meet for lunch now and again, things like that—and all I could think of was how often people will make promises like that and not keep them. Oh they mean to, but they hardly ever do.

"Then, at this afternoon's story hour, my preschoolers gave me a present they'd chipped in for, and some of them cried when we said good-bye. Until then, I guess I hadn't realized how close I'd become to some of the children—how much a part of my life they were—"

Her eyes misted over, and when she faltered into silence, Louis murmured, "This I can understand." He pressed his handkerchief into her hand and patted her shoulder sympathetically. In a jovial tone, he inquired, "Do you know what I'm going to do, Darcy? I'm going to tell Yvette to ease up on you."

"Please, that's not necessary."

"I believe it is," Louis insisted. "Yvette has been known to become overzealous on occasion, and from the looks of you, it appears she's forgotten you're several inches shorter than the average model. Every pound you lose is more noticeable than it would be with a taller woman. How much have you lost?"

"About seven pounds the last time I weighed."

"That's enough," Louis said decisively. "We don't want you too thin. Now, how did you get along with Jere Winston?"

Darcy recalled the imperious way the photographer had dealt with her and a flutter of nerves gripped the pit of her stomach.

"To tell you the truth, I'm not sure," she replied. "I can only tell you that I thought Mr. Winston was terribly knowledgeable."

"And a bit overpowering?" Louis supplied, grinning.

She attempted a smile. "Just a bit."

"Rather like confronting a firing squad?"

"Exactly!" She was laughing now. "But his pictures of me were fabulous!"

Louis nodded agreement. "Do you feel you can work with him?"

"Maybe you should ask Mr. Winston if he can work with me," she suggested diffidently. "Madame Perrigo says he's one of the best."

"He is, and we're fortunate he was available, but please don't be intimidated by his reputation or his manner. I won't tell you Jere's bark is worse than his bite because his bite can be venomous, but he told me he was delighted with your looks and your responsiveness to direction. He feels you have great potential. Does that take some of the pressure off?"

"Yes, it does."

"Good!" Louis said approvingly. "Then since Monday is going to be a brutal day for you, my orders for this weekend are that you're to relax. I want you to continue with the exercises, but forget about your classes, and try to forget that you're facing Jere Winston and his cameras on Monday. Do something you enjoy."

Chapter 10

DO SOMETHING YOU ENJOY. The last of Louis's instructions sang through Darcy's mind as she returned to her apartment. When she stopped at the supermarket, she breezed past the displays of diet foods. She paused at the dairy case to get a quart of milk, but she ignored the neatly aligned cartons of yogurt. Instead, she opted for a steak and a package of frozen hash browns. Her refrigerator was well stocked with the lettuce and other salad vegetables that were the staples of the diet Yvette had drawn up for her, but she added a jar of Roquefort dressing to her provisions before she turned her cart toward the checkout counter.

She felt a twinge of guilt while she waited for the steak to broil and the potatoes to brown. Then Louis's words echoed through her mind and she sat down to eat her hastily prepared meal with a sharp appetite and a clear conscience.

It was only seven thirty when she finished dinner, but she could barely keep her eyes open. She made herself rinse and stack the dishes before she prepared for bed. After she'd showered and gotten into her nightgown, she automatically wound the clock before she remembered that for two marvelous days she needn't submit to the tyranny of the alarm.

This was the last thought she was conscious of. She crawled into bed and was asleep the second her head touched the pillow.

Darcy slept late the next day. She loafed around the apartment for what remained of the morning, and she spent the early afternoon swimming and sunbathing beside the building's pool.

So far she had not permitted thoughts of Jordan to intrude and spoil her weekend, but when she went inside the telephone seemed to mock her with its silence. She took the receiver off the hook and, feeling somewhat better for having taken this preventive action, put a stack of records on the stereo, stretched out on the sofa, and promptly fell asleep.

When she awoke to the measured cadences of Mozart and the lengthening shadows of evening, she felt completely restored. After she'd had an eye-opening cup of coffee, she was filled with an energy so boundless it was almost a pleasure to get into her exercise togs and go through her workout.

She had limbered up, run several miles on the treadmill, and was bouncing on the trampoline to the lively rhythms of a Chuck Mangione recording when the doorbell rang. She jogged to the door without missing a beat, mopping her face with the towel she had draped around her neck as she went. She continued running in place as she opened the door, but she froze when she discovered the identity of her caller.

"Oh, my Lord!" she cried. "Oh, my *Lord!*"

"You needn't address me so formally, Goldilocks,"

he teased. "Just plain Jordan will do."

Darcy's breasts were heaving as she gasped for air. She wished she could bury her head in the towel to hide her flushed, perspiring face and the wild disarray of her hair. She was too taken aback to object when Jordan stepped into the living room without waiting for her invitation.

"Wh-why didn't you call before you came over?" she complained feebly.

"I tried to, but your line was busy."

"What are you doing here?"

"I thought I'd take you out to dinner, unless you've given up eating." Jordan's voice softened and dropped an octave as he added, "I've missed you, Goldilocks."

"I—I've missed you too," she said shyly.

He grinned as if he were pleased by her response and closed the door behind himself. For a moment he stood with his head cocked to one side, looking down at her inquisitively. Then his smile faded and his hands fastened around her waist, measuring its circumference within the span of his fingers.

"I can count your ribs!" he exclaimed. "What the hell have you done to yourself?"

"I've b-been getting in shape," she stammered breathlessly.

"What was wrong with the shape you had before?"

"Nothing I suppose, but the camera adds weight and Yvette wanted to see more of my bone structure."

Jordan ran his forefinger along the new fragility of her cheekbone. "Yvette should be very happy," he said harshly.

He glanced around the room, taking note of the trampoline and treadmill. By the time his eyes returned to her, the critical look had left them and they were shining with barely suppressed amusement.

"Do you have some guy stashed away in the bedroom?" he asked. When she stared at him dumbly, he explained, "What I want to know is, does all your heavy breathing mean I've come at an awkward time, or did I interrupt your workout?"

"Both," she snapped.

Under the impetus of his teasing, Darcy's embarrassment had given way to self-annoyance that he'd caught her wearing the scruffy old leotard and legwarmers she should have scrapped years ago. But Jordan only laughed at her response. She remained rooted to her spot by the door while he stepped around her and strode across the room to the sofa.

As he sat down, he prompted, "Do I smell coffee?"

"I doubt it," she replied curtly. "All I have on hand is instant."

"If I apologize for coming over without phoning first, may I have a cup?"

"Will you apologize for gloating, too?"

"Gloating!" Jordan's injured tone was belied by the "I told you so" glint in his eyes. "Why should I gloat?"

"Maybe because you were right about my romanticizing modeling."

"Well, Goldilocks, if you're big enough to admit your expectations were unrealistic, I guess I can admit I was gloating."

"You have no reason to," she lied grimly. "I'll admit you were right about modeling being damned hard work, but it's also stimulating. I like it!"

"Bully for you!" Jordan's expression was enigmatic. "And now that you've gotten that out of your system, may I have some coffee?"

"Why not," she said with a shrug. But she spoiled the blasé effect by bolting from the living room.

She ran to the safety of the kitchen, silently lamenting the dirty trick fate had played on her. It was ironic that while she'd hoped modeling would help her acquire a sophisticated gloss that would dazzle Jordan, now that she was with him for the first time in two weeks, she was sweaty and grubby, her hair was every which way, and she hadn't a smidgen of lipstick on.

She felt like weeping, but she managed to produce a semblance of aplomb as she carried Jordan's coffee into the living room.

"Aren't you having any?" he asked.

Darcy shook her head and declared, "I'm going to take a shower."

She sensed that Jordan's eyes were following her every move as she walked toward the bedroom. "Make yourself at home," she said, although she was aware this nicety was unnecessary. He was behaving as if he owned the place! "I won't be long."

She was as good as her word. The Chuck Mangione album was replaced with one by Melissa Manchester, but she had applied lipstick and eyeshadow and changed into a violet-sprigged silk-damask skirt and a Victorian-style blouse of sheerest white linen before the record ended.

Jordan was sitting on his heels looking through the record cabinet when she returned to the living room.

"I found out why your line was busy," he said dryly, "and I put the phone back on the hook."

"Thanks. I'd forgotten about it."

His eyes traveled over her in a way that made her keenly aware of him and her face felt as if it were on fire. When he got to his feet, she immediately presented her back to him, sweeping her hair to the side with one hand so that he could see the row of tiny, cloth-covered buttons that secured the collar of the blouse high around her neck.

"Do you mind giving me a hand with these?" she requested. "I can't quite reach them."

She was disappointed when he fastened the buttons without commenting on her appearance, but it seemed he had saved all his praise for her taste in music.

"You have a fantastic record collection," he said.

"Where did you find the oldies by Benny Goodman and Duke Ellington?"

"They were my father's," Darcy replied in a subdued voice. "Some of them date back to the late forties, but I don't actually play them anymore. They've been re-recorded on cassettes."

"I'd like to hear them," Jordan said softly. "Maybe later tonight you could play them for me."

He'd finished with the last button, and when she turned to face him she was arrested by the unconcealed desire she saw in his eyes. She knew she was promising him something much more intimate than an evening of vintage jazz when she nodded and murmured, "Of course. Later."

She was not acquainted with the restaurant he took her to. It was less than a mile from her apartment, but she had never been there before. For that matter, she gained only the haziest impression of its dimly lighted coziness on that night. She ate the food the waiter placed in front of her, but afterward she had no recollection of what she'd ordered.

Jordan filled her senses to the exclusion of everything else. If he'd seemed in his element at the helm of the *Compass Rose,* he was equally at home in the urban setting of the restaurant. Devastatingly attractive even in frayed cutoffs, he was even more handsome in the impeccably tailored slacks, white shirt, and dark blazer he was wearing now. And if his angular profile was commanding when it was etched against the sky, candlelight was the perfect romantic complement to his lean, strong-boned features.

She marveled at his rare capacity to remain at ease no matter how formal or informal the circumstances, and she couldn't tear her gaze away from him. She drank no more than a single glass of wine with her dinner, but when they left the restaurant, she felt as giddy as if she were intoxicated. A languorous warmth had invaded her limbs and her knees were too shaky to support her. When

Jordan put his arm around her, she leaned against him weakly. She was grateful for his support as he guided her to the car he had rented.

The cool night air was sobering. Suddenly fearful, Darcy wondered what sort of heartaches she was letting herself in for. It seemed she had learned nothing from her experience with Tim. She'd sworn she would never let anyone use her again, yet all Jordan had to do was *look* at her and she found herself poised on the brink of surrender. But if part of her was afraid of giving in to her desire, the other part couldn't bear not giving in, and as it turned out, her respite was all too temporary.

Within minutes they were in her living room and Jordan was standing close behind her, undoing not only the buttons at the neckline of her blouse that he'd fastened a little more than an hour before, but the rest of them as well.

His hands were unsteady and his voice was rough with urgency as he said, "Victorian men must have been a bundle of frustrations if they always had to contend with so damned many buttons before they could make love to their women."

He began kissing the nape of her neck. His warm, moist breath fanned over her skin as his lips moved lower along her spine as it was bared to him. When he had undone the last button, he wound his arms around her and folded her even closer to the taut length of his body. He held her so tightly that she felt the spasm of longing that shook him as acutely as she felt the delicious tremor of anticipation that rippled through her own body.

His hands slid inside the blouse and coasted smoothly over her midriff to find the burgeoning swell of her breasts. A triumphant growl of pleasure escaped him when her body responded to his touch, her nipples swelling to erect, tingling peaks beneath his knowing fingertips.

"You knew this would happen tonight, didn't you, Darcy?" he whispered huskily.

"I-I hoped it would," she replied.

Jordan nuzzled her ear and delved into its recesses with the tip of his tongue, causing another delightful shiver to race along her nerve endings. She turned so that she was facing him, moving her body against his in deliberate provocation, rolling her head to one side to guide his lips to the wildly pulsing hollows at the base of her throat.

"You *knew* it would," he murmured against her skin. His hands cupped her buttocks, lifting her onto her tiptoes and fitting her softness to him so that she could feel the hard surge of his arousal. "You knew it when you chose to wear this blouse. You knew it when you asked me to button it for you."

She moved fractionally away from him, leaning back in the warm circle of his arms so that she could see the passion smoldering in his eyes.

"And did you know this would happen tonight?"

Jordan laughed softly. He pressed his cheek to hers and his arms tightened around her so that he was holding her painfully, wonderfully close. "I knew we'd be lovers from the first moment I saw you at Santino's. And before then—"

His lips were skimming across her cheek, and when they found hers the rest of the sentence was lost, absorbed by her mouth as he kissed her. His lips settled over hers lightly at first, courting her response. But when her own lips parted, the pressure of his mouth increased until he was kissing her hungrily, compelling her to return the sweet feint and parry of his tongue.

Her hands were trapped between them, flattened against his chest. She eased them over his shirtfront, searching until she found an opening, and slipped one hand inside the fabric. She touched him lovingly, relishing his hard muscularity, reveling in the crispness of his hair, the smoothness of his skin, the roughness of his flat male nipples.

In reaction to her explorations, his kiss deepened. His tongue was sensuously stroking hers, darting into the sweetest recesses of her mouth, and her own urgency grew. She felt him trembling, felt his swiftly mounting arousal, and her caresses became bolder. She touched him intimately, and when she heard him groan with the pleasure she was giving him, she was engulfed by a hot wave of desire for him.

As if he sensed that her need rivaled his own, without taking his mouth away from hers, Jordan lifted her in his arms. He held her cradled against his chest while he gradually relinquished his possession of her mouth and carried her into the bedroom. His face was only inches away from her own, but she had to strain to see his features in the dusk. The only source of light in the bedroom was the waning summer twilight.

He set her on her feet and fumbled for the lamp on the nightstand. "I want to see you," he said, his voice thick with passion.

Only after he'd found the lamp and switched it on did he begin undressing her. He removed her blouse and unzipped her skirt slowly, almost reverently, and the tightly leashed intensity of his ardor was oddly disconcerting. Darcy trembled uncontrollably as she stared up at him, wondering if she could keep pace with his demands.

She stood there, incapable of moving unless he willed it, not resisting him but not truly participating, while he took off her skirt and lifted her camisole over her head. It was not until he cupped her bare breasts in his hands that her last reservation was vanquished and she was caught up in the volatile rush of his passion.

His thumbs traced sweet, fiery patterns over her nipples and the delicate eroticism of his touch left her gasping. She was feverish with impatience now, and her hands worked at his clothing as frenziedly as his were working at hers.

They shed the last of their clothes, and in the next instant they were lying on the bed, inflamed by the incendiary contact of naked flesh with naked flesh.

Initially, Darcy heard the endearments Jordan murmured. In a ragged whisper he told her how beautiful she was, how desirable. He told her how much he'd wanted her. Then the pounding rush of blood through her ears drowned out his voice as he made love to her slowly, with an exquisite thoroughness that made her acutely aware of every part of her body.

The way he touched her, the way he kissed her, told her how much the silkiness of her hair and the texture of her skin excited him. She felt as if she were seeing herself for the first time through his eyes, through his fingertips, through his lips, as he learned the fullness of her breasts, the narrowness of her waist, the curve of her hips, the softness of her thighs.

And when he positioned himself above her, his ardor transported her to undreamed worlds of ecstasy. She responded mindlessly, opening her thighs to receive him, giving herself to him without restraint, following wherever he led her. With every demanding thrust of his hips, she plunged deeper into a molten sea of sensuality until, at last, she entered a timeless realm where, with the mingling of their bodies and the melding of their souls, they redefined reality.

At the moment of release only the two of them seemed real to Darcy. Her world was transformed, and Jordan encompassed all of it. Reality was the taste of his kiss and the scent of his hair and the silky friction of his skin rubbing against hers. His body heat was the sun, and when she opened her eyes and saw the austere beauty of his face poised above her, the infinite blue of his eyes was heaven.

Reality was the delicious burden of his weight pressing her into the bedclothes, his head resting against her breast. It was the sound of his voice sighing her name, murmuring, "Oh, Goldilocks, you're something special."

I love you, Jordan, she thought, but she didn't say it aloud. She translated the words into the tender way she smoothed the damp strands of hair away from his forehead. She said she loved him with the enraptured smile she gave him.

The smile he gave her in return was a radiant gift that stole her breath away.

They lay in one another's arms while drowsiness overtook them. Just before she dozed off, Darcy thought she heard Jordan whisper, "You're worth waiting for, Goldilocks. For weeks, for years—forever."

A smile touched the corners of her mouth. She fell asleep feeling utterly fulfilled, and happier than she'd ever felt before.

Chapter 11

THE SOFT CLICK of the bedroom door closing wakened Darcy. She half opened her eyes and smiled as memories of Jordan's lovemaking rushed to the surface of her mind, bringing with them a pervasive sense of contentment. But her bubble of elation burst when she reached out for him and found that his side of the bed was empty.

She rolled over and buried her face in the indentation his head had made in the pillow. It was still warm.

For a time she lay still, inhaling the lingering scent of his shaving soap on the pillow case, listening for some further sound that might indicate his presence, praying that he hadn't left the apartment. Then she heard the swish of the living room draperies being opened, and her prayer changed to one of thanksgiving.

Her spirits were soaring again as she got out of bed and slipped into her cotton kimono. She was so eager to see Jordan, to be with him, that she didn't stop to comb her hair or put on her slippers before she left the bedroom. She was still rather groggy, though. Just inside the living room she paused, yawning and rubbing the sleep from her eyes.

Jordan was standing by the window, looking down into the central courtyard around which the apartment complex was built. Although the eastern sky was just turning opalescent with the first light of dawn, he was fully dressed except for his blazer.

"You're up awfully early," she said. "It can't be much later than five thirty."

Jordan started at the sound of her voice, and when he spun around, she saw that he'd even put on his necktie. It was slightly askew and only loosely knotted, but she felt a cold frisson of alarm at the sight of it.

"Is something wrong?" she asked.

"I'm sorry I woke you," he said.

He hadn't answered her question and his tone was oddly reserved, but she reassured herself that he was only tired. He had shifted his stance so that the light coming through the window fell upon his face, and she could see the stubble of beard along his jaw and the shadows beneath his eyes.

She hurried to his side and touched his arm. "Did you sleep at all?"

"I guess I've gotten out of the habit of sleeping ashore," Jordan replied gruffly. "And it doesn't help that my conscience is bothering me."

His grave expression added to her sense of foreboding, but she chose to ignore it, suggesting lightly, "They say confession is good for the soul."

"It's not my soul I'm worried about, Darcy. It's us—you and me. After last night I've decided I have to tell you something, and I'm not sure you'll understand."

Capturing her hand within the grip of his much larger one, he laced his fingers with hers and squeezed them tightly, as if he were afraid she might run away.

I love you, Jordan, she thought. I can understand

anything, forgive anything, as long as you keep on holding my hand this way.

All she said aloud, however, was, "You'll never know unless you try me."

For a long moment Jordan studied her. "Okay, here goes," he said flatly. "I've been sailing under false colors with you, Darcy."

"How do you mean?"

"That day at Roche Harbor you jumped to the conclusion that I didn't know your name until you announced you were Ariel's daughter, I knew who you were all along."

"You knew?" Darcy repeated incredulously. "Even that night at Santino's?"

"Even then."

"All right," she said firmly. "So you'd seen a picture of me and you recognized me. That's no big deal. If I make false assumptions, it's no fault of yours. It's certainly nothing for you to lose sleep over."

"But, Darcy, it was more than that—"

"Please, Jordan. I'd rather you didn't say any more!" When he opened his mouth as if to continue, Darcy placed silencing fingers over his lips. "If you're going to tell me you're involved in some scheme of my mother's to get us together, it doesn't make any difference. I don't care about any of that—"

Frowning, Jordan tore her hand away from his mouth. "You're doing it again," he accused.

"Doing what?"

"Jumping to conclusions."

"Is that so terrible?"

"No, Darcy, it isn't." His expression softened as he pressed a kiss into her palm and laid her hand against his cheek. "It's not terrible at all. It's just that it makes it harder for me to explain, and there have already been too many games between us—"

She tried to tug free of his grasp, but he prevented her from doing so. He walked to the sofa, towing her along behind him, and pulled her after him when he sat down.

"Will you please just listen for a few minutes," he said tautly.

Her eyes fell away from his to focus on his manacle-like grip on her wrists. "It seems I don't have any choice."

"Neither have I, Goldilocks. I wish to God I did. I should have leveled with you from the beginning."

She nodded miserably. "I—I'll listen."

"Thank you." Jordan let go of her, but his face was frighteningly solemn. "To begin with, there was a scheme, but it was mine. Your mother's only contribution was as my adviser."

She flinched at this bald statement of fact, but Jordan rushed on. "I never meant to deceive you, Darcy. You have to believe that."

When he paused, obviously expecting some comment from her, she offered token agreement.

"All right. If you say so."

"The truth is," Jordan said gently, "I'd seen more than your picture before we met at Santino's. I'd seen you."

Her hand shook as she massaged her temple. "But we couldn't have met!" she cried. "I'd have remembered."

"We weren't actually introduced."

"Then where—"

"I was at your wedding, Goldilocks."

Jordan hesitated again, but this time Darcy was too stunned to say anything.

"The weekend you and Cummins were married, my— uh, a friend of mine and I happened to drop in on my aunt, and nothing would do but that we come with her to the church—"

"This friend," Darcy interjected. "Was it Sunny Gardiner?"

"As a matter of fact, it was."

Her hand fell limply to her lap. "According to Yvette Perrigo, she was more than your friend."

"She was my fiancée."

"You were *lovers!*" Darcy declared hotly. "Why don't you come right out and say it."

Jordan sprang to his feet and began pacing back and forth between the sofa and the window. "Very well, Darcy," he said brusquely. "Sunny and I *were* lovers. But we were friends first—from the time we were in high school."

"Are you still lovers?"

Jordan shook his head. "That was over several years ago, but I hope we're still friends." He stopped pacing long enough to glower down at her. "Did Yvette have anything else to say about Sunny and me?"

"She said you'd drifted apart."

"Did she hazard a guess as to why?" he demanded.

Her show of bravado exhausted, Darcy sank weakly into the corner of the couch. "She thought it was because you were separated by your work."

"Yvette might be a walking almanac, but she's wrong on that count." Jordan smiled sardonically and resumed his angry pacing. "It's a relief to know her crystal ball isn't infallible."

"What came between Sunny and you, then?"

"Several things," Jordan answered abstractedly. "The *Compass Rose,* for one."

What else, Darcy thought ruefully.

"All the years when I was working at the boatyard seven days a week, I dreamed about building my own sailboat," Jordan went on. "I talked about it often enough that Sunny knew I hoped to incorporate some of my grandfather's ideas in the design of the boat. She knew how I felt about Grandpop, too, and I never made any secret of the fact that I was determined to do everything in my power to see that he got the recognition he deserved. But Sunny thought it was only a pipe dream. Not that she told me this. Whenever we'd talk about the future, she just went along with whatever I suggested. Since she didn't believe I'd ever do anything but talk about having my own boat, she probably didn't see any harm in humoring me, but the upshot was I thought we wanted the same things."

"And you didn't," Darcy said tonelessly.

"No. Far from it. Her plans called for me to sell the business and move into the city. To show you how out of sync we were, she thought I'd be happy clipping coupons while she pursued her career as a model, and I thought she'd be relieved to sign on as my first mate and get away from the razzle-dazzle of that world for a few years.

"Then work got under way on my boat, and Sunny realized I actually intended to carry out my plans for an around-the-world cruise when the *Compass Rose* was launched. That was when things started to go sour between us. She began to resent the amount of time I spent working on the boat, she resented the *Compass Rose*—she even resented Grandpop, and he'd been dead quite a few years by then."

Jordan's pacing had slowed. Finally, he sat down in the corner of the sofa opposite Darcy's. She watched him obliquely as he made himself comfortable, resting his head against the upholstery at his back and stretching his long legs out in front of him. Her chest felt tight with disappointment because he'd chosen to sit so far away from her.

"My aunt used to say that Sunny was the kind of person who wants to be the bride at every wedding and the corpse at every funeral," he said thoughtfully. "That's a gross overstatement of course, but Sunny used to get jealous of her maid if the poor woman wanted to earn a little extra money by moonlighting occasionally, so I probably should have foreseen how she'd react to my preoccupation with the *Compass Rose*. Sunny wanted my undivided attention—she needed it, I guess—and when I couldn't give it to her, we decided we'd be better off apart. Each of us had our own goals, and they were diametrically opposed—"

Jordan went on in this vein, but Darcy heard almost

nothing of what he said. She tried to remain attentive, but her mind kept returning to the revelation that he was going to sail around the world on the *Compass Rose*.

"When will you be leaving?" she asked.

"As soon as they've finished filming the commercial," he replied. "I promised Yvette and Louis I'd stick around till then."

Once she learned this, Darcy derived little satisfaction from having effectively sidetracked the conversation. She hadn't wanted Jordan to talk about the two of them. She knew he didn't love her, and she couldn't have endured his letting her down gently. She couldn't bear listening to him say all the polite and proper things as to why there could never be anything permanent about their relationship without bursting into tears, and if he told her one more time that she was "a good kid," she would scream. But this was worse!

She wondered how long he would be gone. Didn't a circumnavigation take years?

As Jordan spoke, it became increasingly apparent that he was staunchly committed to his plan. He'd already taken steps to publicize his grandfather's innovations. One of the better known yachting magazines had agreed to publish the articles he submitted about his travels.

"It would be great to come home with enough material to write a book about the trip," he said, "but it's unlikely I will. There have been so many successful voyages in small boats that books about sailing are old hat unless you're a famous personality or you cross the Pacific single-handed in a ten footer—or you're shipwrecked."

The thought of Jordan being shipwrecked made Darcy's heart race with anxiety. She wanted to plead with him, "Don't go. It's much too risky. If anything were to happen to you—"

She couldn't bear to finish this thought. The idea of living in a world without Jordan was too dreadful to contemplate.

"Damn it all!" Jordan's harsh imprecation roused

Darcy from her maudlin inertia. "How the hell did I get started on this subject when it's you and me I want to talk about!"

Before he could say anything more, Darcy leaped to her feet. Relying on her instincts, she sauntered across the room with an exaggerated swing of her hips and positioned herself at the window so that the rays of the rising sun outlined her body through the thin cotton of her kimono.

She realized that this was her last resort, and hoping the diversion would work, she sucked in her breath so that her breasts assumed an especially provocative tilt before she swiveled around to face him.

In a throaty murmur she asked, "Do you know what I thought when I first saw you standing on the roof of my mother's garage?"

"Darcy—" Jordan's eyes swept over her avidly, widening when they arrived at the enticing thrust of her breasts and the feminine curve of her hips. She knew her ploy was having the desired effect from the agitated way his throat worked when he swallowed.

She moistened her lips, smiled a Gioconda smile, and let her own gaze stray suggestively over his body. His physical arousal was becoming more evident by the second. His eyes were heavy-lidded with desire when he raised them to hers.

She started walking toward him, her body swaying sinuously, and when she reached him, she settled herself in his lap, seductively wriggling her hips against his.

"Damn it all, Darcy!" he muttered thickly. "We have to talk."

"But, Jordan, that's what we've been doing. You've been talking, and I've been listening. Now it's my turn." Looping her arms around his neck, she trailed kisses along his jawline to his ear.

"When I first saw you," she whispered, "I wondered if you'd look as magnificent without your clothes as in them." She caught his earlobe between her teeth and nipped at it playfully. "Now I know you do."

A shaky chuckle rumbled out from deep in Jordan's chest, encouraging her to cover the side of his neck with moist butterfly kisses.

In the same velvety rumble he asked, "Do you want to know what I thought when I first saw you?"

Darcy nodded dreamily, loving the raspy feel of his beard against her cheek.

"I wondered if you were a natural blonde." His voice was gravelly with emotion and his hands were impatient as he untied the belt of her kimono. "Now I know you are."

She bit her lip to keep from crying out her pleasure as Jordan's hands slid inside the robe. In the next instant he was caressing her intimately with one hand, while the other was spread hotly between her shoulder blades, arching her toward him as he bent his head to her breasts. His mouth followed the rise of one breast to its crest, and when his lips fastened about the nipple, it ripened wantonly within the moist circling of his tongue.

"Don't think you'll get away with this indefinitely, Goldilocks," he murmured around the sensitive shell-pink bud, "because I know what you're up to." He raised his head and cupped her chin with his hand, tilting her face toward his. "You've been trying to distract me, but you're only postponing the inevitable. Eventually, you'll have to listen to the truth—"

"Hush, darling." She pulled his head down to hers and silenced him with a kiss. Her lips moved invitingly against his as she teased, "I'm not shopping for Cuisinarts or wedding rings, and I'm not asking for any guarantees. All I want is your body."

She had already tossed his necktie to the far end of the sofa, and now she began unbuttoning his shirt. He inhaled raggedly at the tantalizing brush of her hands upon his skin, and his arms clamped around her possessively.

"You win, Darcy," he growled. "This time we'll do

it your way—but only because I want you too damned much to argue about it."

He hugged her to him with breathtaking ardor and, with a lithe twist of his body, tumbled her off his lap so that she was sprawled beneath him on the sofa. His mouth came down on hers in a plundering, ravishing kiss. Both of them were writhing, straining to be even closer, and for a blissful time arguments were forgotten.

The morning sky grew brighter and sunbeams flooded through the windowpanes, drenching the living room and bathing them in a pool of light, but Darcy didn't notice. She and Jordan were wrapped in rapturous bonds of passion, locked together in an erotic craving that transcended all other needs, as they made love with a lusty, almost primitive, abandon.

Chapter **12**

HAD JORDAN BELIEVED her claim that her only interest
in him was sexual, Darcy asked herself sometime later.

It seemed he had, because although they spent most
of that Sunday together, he didn't try to bring up the
subject of their relationship again. Darcy didn't know
whether she should be proud of her convincing performance or insulted because he'd so readily accepted her
words at face value.

They slept late into the morning, showered and dressed,
went out for brunch, and returned to her apartment to
read the newspaper and listen to the stereo. The day
passed all too quickly, and when it was over her feelings
about it were a confused mingling of pleasure and pain.

Before the end of the week they would have finished
filming the commercial on the *Compass Rose*. Then Jordan would go off on his cruise, and she would be left to
pick up the pieces of her foolish heart.

Why had she fallen in love with him, she wondered. He didn't love her. He didn't need her. He almost never paid her pretty compliments the way Tim had. He was impossibly arrogant and implacably single-minded.

If his most casual touch made her go weak-kneed with wanting him, that didn't mean she had to be weak-headed as well. Why couldn't she satisfy her sexual urges with him and let it go at that?

That afternoon they watched one of her parents' old movies on television, and in the course of the telecast, Darcy discovered at least one reason why she longed for more than a short-lived affair with Jordan.

It was not one of Ariel and Darryl's better movies. It was really only a grade-B tearjerker, and she had seen it a dozen times before, but she still found the poignant ending deeply moving.

When Jordan saw that she was crying, he didn't joke about her tears as some men might have. He didn't ridicule the film and criticize its technical aspects as Tim would have. Jordan simply handed her a box of tissues and went into the kitchen to refill their coffee mugs, leaving her alone to indulge her sentiments to her heart's content.

These were small, seemingly unimportant acts, but suddenly Darcy knew why she loved Jordan so much.

Jordan cares about people, she thought. He cared enough to bring her a cup of coffee and assess the roof of Ariel's house. He cared enough to balance checkbooks for his aunt and sail around the world for his grandfather.

And if his response to her tears reflected his practical approach to life, it also demonstrated that he respected her feelings. And since Jordan acknowledged her right to be hopelessly romantic, shouldn't she feel free to relax with him, to let down her guard and be herself?

Her thoughts wandered back to the night at Santino's, and she recalled that from their very first encounter she had been impressed by Jordan's directness. She remembered the day on the *Compass Rose* when he'd told her there were times when directness was much more effective than cleverness. She remembered that only that morning he'd said, "There have already been too many games between us," and she realized that she never should have tried to mislead him.

She should have told him she loved him and they could have gone on from there. They might even have corresponded during the years he would be away on his voyage. But though she recognized the soundness of this approach, Darcy knew she could never have risked it. The scars left by Tim's manipulation and rejection of her were only just healed, and if Jordan had declined her love, the old wounds would only have opened anew, perhaps never to close again.

Jordan left soon after this. Their original plan called for him to check on the *Compass Rose*, pick up a change of clothes, then come back. They were to have dinner together and he would spend the night with her. But shortly after his arrival at Shilshole Bay Marina, he telephoned to tell her he wouldn't be able to keep their date.

"The harbormaster's been looking for me since yesterday afternoon." His voice was vibrant with barely contained excitement as he said, "They've delivered the figurehead."

"The what?" she asked.

"The figurehead for the *Compass Rose,*" he replied. "The script for the TV commercial calls for the figurehead to come to life and—oh, hell! I can't explain it, but I don't want to leave until it's properly installed."

"Then you must stay there," Darcy said dully.

"I knew I could count on you, Goldilocks. You're a damned good sport!"

"I'm sorry you can't come back, though," she admitted. "I'll miss you."

"I'll miss you, too," Jordan said softly. "I wish I could be with you tonight, but maybe it's best that I can't."

"H-how do you mean?" Darcy asked tremulously.

"Well, tomorrow's your big day. You'll want to get a good night's sleep, and you wouldn't if I were there."

His velvety chuckle reminded her of their lovemaking, and she laughed with him, tacitly agreeing that neither of them was likely to do much sleeping if they were sharing the same bed.

"Will you come to Mr. Winston's studio tomorrow?" she asked. "It would mean a lot to me if you were there."

"Surely you're not nervous about posing for him!"

"Yes, I guess I am a little nervous," she answered hesitantly. "Actually, I'm more than a little nervous." She laughed again, a bit shakily this time, and confessed, "What I am is petrified!"

"You'll be just fine, Darcy," Jordan said firmly. He sounded so positive that she almost believed him. "I know you won't need me, but if it'll make you feel better, I'll be happy to come."

As she hung up the phone, Darcy thought, You're wrong, Jordan. I will need you tomorrow. I'll need you even more than I do tonight. I'll never get over needing you.

Chapter 13

THE LIGHT IN the studio was glaring, the fans were blowing a gale, the stereo was blaring, Jere Winston was shouting, and his camera was clicking away.

It was only a little after five o'clock, but to Darcy it seemed more like midnight.

She had reported to the hairdresser at seven o'clock sharp, just as Yvette had ordered. Her hair was shampooed, conditioned, rinsed, and set on oversize rollers. Then the cosmetician took over. After deliberating whether her eyebrows should be bleached or reshaped, he opted to leave them as they were, but for the next hour her face was cleansed and creamed, painted and highlighted, blushed and shaded with palest beiges, taupes, peaches, and corals until her features were so recontoured by the subtle layering of makeup that she hardly recognized herself in the pouting, sloe-eyed temptress who stared back at her from the hand mirror the makeup man held.

The hairdresser returned to remove the rollers and

comb out her hair. He'd styled it so that it trailed down her back, tumbling loosely about her shoulders in a silken silver-gold cloud. Although he'd taken three times as long as she would have, her hair didn't look markedly different than it had when she'd walked into the studio.

At nine thirty Yvette appeared. She gave her stamp of approval to the work the hairdresser and makeup artist had done and shooed them out of the dressing room.

"So, *ma petite,*" she said, "the transformation is almost complete, *n'est-ce pas?*"

"Is Jordan here?" Darcy inquired anxiously.

"Yes, he is. He arrived a few minutes after Louis and me." Yvette looked faintly surprised, but she was all business and in much too much of a rush to ask Darcy questions about her obvious need for Jordan's presence. She hurried to the wardrobe rack and removed one of the costumes. Holding the sequin-banded gold-and-apricot harem-pants outfit at arms length she announced dramatically, "We start with this."

Darcy slipped out of her smock and Yvette zipped her into the hip-hugging trousers. While Darcy got into the skimpy matching bra and brief bolero, Yvette unlocked a leather case and selected some topaz-studded gold slave bracelets from a glittering array of jewelry.

"Take care not to misplace these," she cautioned as she handed the bracelets to Darcy. "They're the real McCoy."

The colloquialism was unexpected and humorous coming from Yvette's lips. Smiling, Darcy turned the sparkling bangles this way and that as she slid them over her wrists and onto her forearms. The lustrous detail of the beaten gold setting was delightful, and she admired the way the light struck amber fires in the depths of the emerald-cut gemstones.

"These must be worth a small fortune!" she exclaimed.

"They are," Yvette confirmed, "but a security guard is posted at the door, so you needn't be overly concerned about wearing them."

Darcy buckled the gold kid slippers that completed her ensemble, and she was ready. She would have stopped to admire her appearance in the full-length mirror, but Yvette was already propelling her through the door. As they entered the studio, Yvette dropped behind her.

"Voilà!" she called, and everyone in the cavernous room dropped whatever they were doing to stare at Darcy. Her entrance elicited a smattering of applause and even a few whistles.

"Egad, Yvette!" Jere Winston cried. "You've taken this pretty young lady and created a veritable odalisque!"

"That was the general idea," said Louis.

Darcy had hoped she'd have a chance to see Jordan, but it soon became apparent this was not to be. Yvette hustled her into the ring of lights, and the hairdresser scurried toward her, brandishing his styling brush. Then the makeup man was there with his powderbrush and, at the same time, Yvette was introducing her to the male model.

"This handsome devil is Eric Laurence." She jockeyed Darcy closer to the tall, handsome man and stepped back to study them together. *"Eh bien!* Do they not make a gorgeous couple, Louis?"

"They do," Louis agreed. "Eric's just the right height for Darcy. She won't have to stand on a telephone book after all."

"Dar-cee is wearing four-inch heels," Yvette pointed out.

"Too bad Eric's only a prop," said Jere. "You're sure you don't want to feature him as well?"

"Positive!" Yvette and Louis chorused.

"Certainly not," Miles added his veto as he joined them. "We want it just the way we planned it. It will be perfect that way. Absolutely perfect." Darcy had to bite her lip to suppress a laugh as Miles produced his habitual tagline.

While the four of them conferred over last-minute details, Darcy scanned the studio. She tried to spot Jordan, but the lights were so blinding that she could distinguish only the vague shadowy forms of the onlookers. Then Eric said, "I'm sorry, but I didn't catch your name," and she had to answer him.

"Do you know what this is all about?" he asked.

"It's supposed to be pure fantasy," Darcy began, but before she could say anything more, the conference ended. Louis, Yvette, and Miles moved away, and Jere shouted peremptorily, "Quiet! Quiet, everyone!"

Draping one arm about Darcy's shoulders, he said, "Now, listen up, sweetie. You know that for this one Eric's rubbed his magic lamp—" He stopped abruptly and bellowed, "Toby! Where the hell is the lamp?"

"Got it, Jere," answered a disembodied voice from a far corner of the room.

A moment later the assistant appeared with a reproduction of an antique oil lamp that looked so authentic that it might have come straight from Aladdin's cave. After Toby had positioned the lamp on a waist-high crate that was swathed with a length of red velvet, Jere nodded his approval and Toby vanished back into the shadows.

"Now, where was I?" said Jere.

"I'd just rubbed my magic lamp," Eric prompted.

"Ah, yes, so you had! And when your genie appears, you ask for champagne. But not just any champagne." Jere interrupted his narrative to give Darcy a villainous ogle. "You demand the very best, Eric—witness this delectable little houri—and the very best champagne is—"

"Perrigo's!" Miles enthusiastically supplied the advertising slogan. *"The* champagne for any occasion."

"Gotcha," Eric said dryly.

"Go to the head of the class!" Jere cheered. "As for you, Darcy, Eric is your lord and master, and you love him madly. When I say the word, I want you to look at him as if anything he asks for is his. You adore the guy, right?"

"Right," Darcy parroted doubtfully, wondering how

she could express all that with a man she'd met only five minutes before. Especially when her heart belonged completely to Jordan Ives.

"Just reach down deep inside yourself, sweetie, and give it all you've got," Jere advised. Then, turning to his assistant, he shouted, "Toby! Where's the champagne?"

"Comin' right up, boss."

Jere frowned and stalked away from them. A cork exploded, and a few seconds later he stepped back into the light, carrying an unopened magnum of champagne in one hand and a Lalique goblet in the other. He arranged the bottle in the folds of velvet beside the oil lamp and handed the glass of champagne to Eric.

"That's to look at, fella, not to drink," he instructed, wagging his finger at Eric before he strode off into the shadows calling, "Music, Toby!"

Today, perhaps to evoke the appropriate mood, Jere had put Rimsky-Korsakov's *Scheherezade* on the tape deck. For the next few minutes he peered at Darcy and Eric through his viewfinder and made minute adjustments to the reflectors and the overhead scrims that would enable him to capture the texture of Darcy's fair hair in his photographs. The key light was trained upon her, casting Eric into the shadows, and when Jere wasn't calling out directions to them as to how they should pose, he hummed and tapped his foot in time to the "Sultana's Theme."

His perpetual motion tuned Darcy's apprehensions to a fine pitch. Her stomach had clenched into a tight knot, her hands were clammy, and despite the heat of the lights, she began to shiver.

"There's nothing to be nervous about," Eric encouraged her in an undertone only she could hear. "Jere's a fussbudget, but he knows what he's doing. He'll make you look sensational."

"It's not Jere I'm afraid of," she murmured.

"Well, I hope it's not me."

Darcy shook her head. She felt horribly insecure because she knew Jordan was standing somewhere in the shadows, watching. When she'd asked him to come she'd thought only of how she needed his emotional support, but now she remembered the thinly veiled contempt with which he'd referred to the "razzle-dazzle" of the modeling world. Seeing her at the center of this world was hardly likely to endear her to him.

She shook her head again, vigorously, attempting to clear it of these troublesome thoughts, and her flying hair brought the hairdresser at the gallop.

"Leave it!" Jere raised his voice to make himself heard above the music. "It looks softer when it's mussed. If it's too bad, it can be fixed in retouching." Without straightening from his crouch behind the camera, he ordered, "Give her something to blot her forehead with, though. Get's kind of hot under the lights, doesn't it, sweetie?"

"Yes, it does," she said faintly. She dabbed carefully at her face and throat with the cool cloth the makeup man provided. When she had finished, Jere called, "Toby! Get in there with the light meter."

Toby came running, Jere muttered something unintelligible about his f-stop, and with that the shoot had gotten well and truly under way.

In the hours since then, Darcy had been photographed in several different costumes and as many moods; serene and languorous and oozing vivacity. She'd changed from the harem pants to an elegant white satin evening gown with chiffon panels that floated out behind her like gossamer wings in the breeze from the fans. From the evening dress she'd changed to gold suede culottes, a coordinated fringed vest, a tailored white shirt, a gaucho hat, and boots for what Yvette called "a sportive look."

Her hair had been threaded with ribbons and wreathed with flowers and feathers. It had been styled in a psyche knot and braided. Her makeup was replenished, then toned down. She'd been photographed in flat light and crosslight and backlight, wrapped in sable and dripping diamonds and pearls.

Using a filter of sheerest *mousseline de soie*, Jere softened the lighting and made some diffused shots to accentuate her bone structure and turn the sparkle in her eyes to stars.

"Lift your chin, sweetie!" he told her, and she did. "Bend you knee a bit and point your toe toward the camera. No! The other foot," he told her, and she did. "Touch his hair—lots of feeling now," Jere told her. "Think sweet," he told her. "Think sexy. Give it everything you've got!"

She ran her fingers through Eric's hair, but it was Jordan she thought of. She thought of kissing Jordan, of making love with him, and she smiled at Eric with so much longing, she looked at him with such melting compliance, that Jere rhapsodized, "Dynamite, sweetie! Simply marvelous! We'll set the film on fire with these!"

When Jere stopped to reload his camera, Eric said, "I knew you could do it, Darcy. Beneath that cool exterior beats the heart of a passionate woman."

Darcy finally got to say hello to Jordan when they broke for lunch, but even then she was surrounded by people, and their meeting was less than satisfactory.

"You and Eric seem to be enjoying yourselves," Jordan observed dispassionately. He smiled mechanically and his eyes were wintry. If she hadn't known better, she might have mistaken his coolness for jealousy. But she realized Jordan hadn't stopped by the dressing room for the sole purpose of seeing her when he flagged down Louis as he passed by.

"If you have the time today," he said, "I'd like you to take a look at the figurehead."

"Is it already in place?" Louis inquired with some surprise.

"It was delivered this weekend," Jordan replied. "I'm

really pleased with the way it turned out." As the two men walked away, Darcy overheard Jordan saying, "As long as you're running ahead of schedule with the pictures for the print ads, I wonder if it would be feasible to move up the filming—"

They walked out of hearing range just then, so she couldn't hear the rest of Jordan's request, but her heart was heavy with the certainty that he hoped to leave Seattle as soon as possible.

Over the next half-hour the others drifted out of the dressing room. At last only Darcy and Yvette remained.

As she handed Darcy a container of yogurt, Yvette said, "Do you think you can manage without me for a while? I'm supposed to meet Louis and Jordan for lunch at The Wharf in twenty minutes."

"You needn't worry about me," Darcy replied evenly. "I'll be fine."

"I know you will." Yvette smiled confidently. "You're doing beautifully, and you're in the best of hands with Jere. It's only that we're going to try to work out a new taping date for the commercial, so I may not be back till late this afternoon."

"I heard Jordan say something about that to Louis."

"Yes," said Yvette. "If we can arrive at an accommodation with the crew and if the weatherman cooperates, Jordan would like us to do the location shots on board his boat the day after tomorrow. I gather he's anxious to get away."

"I see." Darcy peeled the lid off the yogurt carton and absently stirred the contents with a plastic spoon. "All we have left for today is the bikini outfit, isn't it?"

"That's right." Yvette began tidying the jewelry away in the leather case, storing bracelets, rings, and necklaces in their fitted, velvet-lined compartments. "Jere would also like to try some simpler shots, without the makeup and without the high heels."

"What about my height?"

"He claims he can stretch you out with his camera."

Darcy tried to laugh, but her laughter was strained. "That sounds like quite a trick."

"I know," Yvette agreed, "but Jere swears he can make you look four inches taller than you are." She shut the clasps on the jewel case and twirled the dials to lock it. As she hefted the case, she said, "It will be a relief to get this back to the jewelers." She collected her shoulder bag and started toward the door, but at the last moment she turned to look at Darcy.

"I cannot begin to tell you," she said quietly, "how much Louis and I appreciate the way you've taken hold of this assignment, Dar-cee. You have surpassed our highest expectations."

Yvette's expression of gratitude was very nearly Darcy's undoing. Feeling like the world's worst fraud, she bent her head over her cup of yogurt and stirred it furiously, fighting to hold back tears.

"Please, Madame Perrigo," she replied with only a slight stammer, "d-don't mention it."

"Very well, *ma petite,* be modest if you must," Yvette gaily allowed. "But we will be still be grateful." Then, with a gamine grin and a cheerful *"A bientôt,"* she was gone.

Darcy forced herself to eat a few spoonfuls of the yogurt before she replaced the cap on the carton and tossed it into the wastebasket. She felt numb, too apathetic for self-pity, and she was unaware she was crying until a tear fell hotly on the back of her hand.

A few minutes later, Toby knocked at the dressing room door. He advised her that Jere was almost ready to resume the sitting and she was thankful that she had to concentrate on applying an even coat of body makeup and getting into the honey-colored silk-jersey bikini.

She tried to erase thoughts of Jordan and think of nothing but adjusting the long, narrow, deeply slit wraparound skirt so that it clung to her hips and exposed just the right amount of midriff. The hot-orange poppies that bloomed about the hem of the skirt were a bit blurry at times, but if she blinked once or twice her vision cleared.

She told herself she'd have plenty of time to grapple with the truth later. After the filming on the *Compass Rose* was completed and Jordan was gone, she'd have all the time in the world to think about where she'd gone wrong. She'd have the rest of her life to yearn for what might have been. But the hollow ache she felt inside as she slipped into cork-soled beach clogs and tucked an artificial poppy behind her ear had nothing to do with the fact that she hadn't finished eating her lunch.

When she returned to the studio, she found that Jere had opened the shades at the windows and lowered the awning over the skylight. Sunlight poured in and was magnified to an almost blinding intensity by the white walls of the room. This gave Darcy a ready excuse when Jere commented on her overbright eyes.

He called out orders and she started posing, but her movements felt brittle, lifeless. They must have looked that way too, because after a little while Jere called a halt.

"The reason I'm using the strobe, sweetie, is so that I can make a lot of very fast exposures," he explained. "I want you to move and give me lots of animation now. More pizzazz. Move, move, move!" he shouted.

She rallied and did her utmost to follow his directions. For the last half-hour she'd been dancing to the incessant disco beat from the stereo; swaying and strutting, bending and dipping. Sometimes her steps flagged momentarily, but when Jere shouted out encouragement, she immediately picked up the tempo. At the end she was lost in frenetic motion. Even when the cassette wound to a stop, she kept on dancing for a few imaginary bars, oblivious to the unaccustomed pall of silence that hung over the studio.

She stopped when she suddenly realized that Jere and

Toby were staring at her as if she'd taken leave of her senses. Maybe I have, she thought numbly.

"The light's about gone, so that's all for today, sweetie," Jere announced briskly. "Unless I'm mistaken, I've got some terrific shots for the campaign."

Darcy left the studio hoping her heightened color would be attributed to the way she'd been exerting herself. She automatically headed for the dressing room, and in the privacy of that haven she collapsed into a chair. She was shaking all over and her breathing was labored. She slumped forward and held her head in her hands until she felt steadier.

When Yvette popped her head through the doorway a few minutes later, Darcy was seated in front of the mirror, smearing cold cream on her face.

"I'm glad I caught you," said Yvette, flashing her engaging grin.

"Was your business meeting productive?" Darcy asked.

"Very! That's why I wanted to speak with you. I've brought your script, and also this." Yvette held up a garment bag as she walked into the room. In a jubilant tone she urged, "Go on! Have a look at it. It's your costume for the commercial."

"Is it all set for Wednesday, then?"

"It's all set—weather permitting. There's a fog rolling in just now." Yvette's smile slackened as she studied Darcy more closely, making a feature by feature appraisal of her face. "But you look so tired, Dar-cee, and I'm sure you must be longing to have a long soak in a hot tub. If you would prefer, we could go over the script at your place."

"To tell the truth, Madame Perrigo, the way I feel just now, I'm afraid if I don't get into a hot bath soon, rigor mortis might set in," Darcy admitted. "I'll only be a minute longer—or if you'd rather, why don't you go on ahead? You can take my key and let yourself into my apartment."

"Certainly, *ma petite,* but would you not like me to drive you home?"

"It's kind of you to offer, but it's not necessary. I have my car here."

"I'll see you at your apartment then. Half an hour?"

"Half an hour," Darcy agreed.

She turned back to the mirror and began wiping away the cold cream, but when she saw that Yvette was still watching her, she raised one eyebrow inquiringly.

"Dar-cee." Yvette spoke rather hesitantly now. "I wonder—how long have you known Jordan?"

Darcy lowered her eyelids to hide the regret that splintered through her at the mention of Jordan's name. "We were introduced that weekend at Roche Harbor," she replied.

Yvette nodded. "I thought so, but it's truly uncanny how much the figurehead resembles you. You might almost have posed for the sculptor."

Darcy raised her eyes slowly, forcing herself to meet Yvette's gaze. The older woman's expression was watchful, her brows knitted with perplexity.

"Shouldn't it?" she reasoned. "After all, it was commissioned for the commercial—"

"But no, *ma petite,*" Yvette interjected sharply. "Jordan ordered the figurehead more than six months ago."

Chapter 14

DEAR LORD, WHAT have I done? The question seemed to thunder through Darcy's mind. Her hands were shaking as she wiped away the last of the cold cream and got into her street clothes.

If she had known where Jordan's boat was moored, she would have gone straight to the marina from the studio, but since she hadn't a clue as to the *Compass Rose*'s exact location, she drove toward her apartment. Looking for the ketch among the thousands of pleasure craft that were tied up at Shilshole Bay would be like searching for a needle in a haystack.

Especially in this fog, thought Darcy when a black sedan suddenly loomed up in front of her car. Her hands tightening on the steering wheel, she eased her foot off the accelerator and leaned forward to look more closely at the street ahead.

Was Yvette right about the figurehead, she wondered. And if Yvette was right, what did that mean?

It was easy to see how much the *Compass Rose* meant to Jordan. The boat represented a link with his grandfather, so it followed that the figurehead would be vitally important to him. He would have given painstaking consideration to its design. But did that mean that *she* was important to him? And what had he wanted to tell her yesterday morning at her apartment? Had he been trying to say he loved her?

As she dodged in and out among the slower-moving traffic, Darcy berated herself for not listening to Jordan. He'd reproached her for jumping to conclusions, and even then she'd refused to listen. If she had heard him out, she wouldn't have to wonder how he felt about her. She would know whether the figurehead's resemblance to her was merely a particularly cruel accident of fate or if Jordan had planned it that way.

"Please, God," she murmured, "don't let it be a coincidence."

She was speeding, driving much too fast for safety through the swirling blanket of fog, but it seemed to take forever before she reached the apartment complex. She parked her car haphazardly and didn't stop to lock it. She ran into the lobby and punched the button for the elevator, then decided she couldn't wait for it and ran up the three flights of stairs to her floor.

The intensive training program Yvette had put her on paid off here. She was only slightly winded when she rang the bell at her apartment, but when her mother opened the door, the remaining air rushed out of her lungs, leaving her speechless with astonishment.

Ariel appeared to be livid about something. She was waving a rectangular slip of paper beneath Darcy's nose and demanding, "What is the meaning of this?"

Darcy's glance darted over Ariel's shoulder as she walked into the living room. She sighed with relief when she saw that Yvette was sitting in one of the club chairs, watching the mother-daughter confrontation with some amusement.

"M-mother, what are you doing here?" Darcy asked breathlessly. Realizing how ungracious this sounded, she added, "Not that this isn't a pleasant surprise, but why didn't you let me know you were coming to Seattle? And by the way, whatever happened to hello?"

"Hello!" Ariel snapped. "I'll give you hello, you little wretch, the moment you've explained why you sent me this—this—" She waved the slip of paper again, and this time Darcy was able to identify it as the check she'd mailed to her mother.

"Well, Mother, I thought—"

"You *thought?*" Ariel cut in hotly. "My darling daughter, if you'd thought, you'd never have sent me this check. If you'd thought about it at all, you'd know I could never, under any circumstances, accept this amount of money from you."

"B-but I thought you needed—"

"Well I don't." Drawing herself to her full height, Ariel proclaimed regally, "I've been a bit strapped for cash because I've been trying to pay off some back taxes, but that's only a temporary situation. I'm on my way to Roche Harbor to list the property there, and once it's sold, I'll get Internal Revenue off my back. But even if it doesn't sell, I'm hardly destitute—and if I were, before I'd let my daughter support me, I'd—I'd sleep in the streets! I'd starve!"

"Brava, Ariel!" said Yvette, and her applause seemed to ring down the curtain on Ariel's melodramatic performance.

Grinning, she dropped a curtsey toward Yvette and another to Darcy. "That was rather effective, wasn't it?" she said. "Now and again it's nice to know I haven't lost my touch."

"Believe me, Mother," Darcy said vehemently, "you haven't lost *anything*."

"Did I really have you convinced?"

Darcy nodded and sank into a chair, and Ariel laid the check on the lamp table at her elbow.

"You have only yourself to blame, darling," she scolded. "When I saw you at Roche Harbor, I tried to reassure you that my financial position is relatively sound, so it was really very bad of you to send me the check. I don't know whether to kiss you or throttle you."

"Don't be too hard on the child," said Yvette. "Perhaps she is seeing many things incorrectly these days. Being in love has a tendency to cloud one's perspective."

Ariel looked at Darcy sharply. "Are you in love, darling?"

"Yes, I am." Darcy met her mother's gaze without flinching. "I'm in love with Jordan."

"Well you needn't sound so huffy about it. I think it's wonderful! I'd hoped you'd have the good sense to recognize how perfect the two of you are for each other." Ariel laughed merrily. "But if you've succumbed to that perfectly yummy young man, why in heaven's name did you tie yourself down with the advertising campaign? I had visions of Jordan and you sailing off into the setting sun and returning home in a year or three to present me with a grandchild!"

"I believe I may be partially responsible for Dar-cee's misreading her cues," said Yvette. "You see, I told her about Sunny Gardiner—"

"Sunny Gardiner!" Ariel sniffed disdainfully. "Jordan began to lose interest in her from the very first moment he saw my daughter."

"I've no doubt he did," Yvette replied equably. "But when I told Dar-cee that Jordan preferred his women glamorous—and I'm afraid I laid it on quite thickly—I genuinely believed this to be the truth. I thought I was doing Dar-cee a good turn." After a brief hesitation Yvette added defensively, "And you're forgetting, Ariel, it was from you she got the mistaken notion you were in need of money."

With a rueful shake of her head Ariel admitted, "You're

right about that, Yvette. It's fairly obvious my daughter has been working on the assumption that there has to be an ulterior motive connected to everything I do. Darryl used to warn me I'd outsmart myself someday, and I guess that day is here, because the truth is that I'd hoped you'd give up searching for a champagne blonde and offer me the assignment as spokesperson for Perrigo Wines."

There was a full minute of stunned silence during which Ariel looked from Darcy to Yvette and back to Darcy again as if she were satisfied that her bombshell had hit its target.

At last, her voice breathy with excitement, Yvette said, "Ariel, you are not—how do you say—putting me on?"

"Certainly not. I never joke about my work."

"Then why did you promote me for the job?" asked Darcy.

"How could I not promote you, darling? When Miles said you were just the blonde they'd been looking for, I couldn't disagree. You're my daughter, and no matter what anyone says, blood is thicker than greasepaint."

"But, Ariel, I'm desolate!" Yvette cried. "If only Louis and I had had some inkling you were interested in working with us! To have the celebrated Ariel St. Denis endorse our wines would have meant much to us, but we had no idea you'd consider coming out of retirement."

"I could tell you a long sad story about my retirement, Yvette, but I'll say only that I never intended to retire permanently. Oh, there were a few months after Darryl's death when I didn't feel up to working. I actually refused a couple of parts I would have been delighted to accept otherwise, and before you could say scat, the myth had gotten started that I'd given up my career. After that, I wasn't offered any worthwhile roles. The only scripts I received were for horror films and TV pilots. I couldn't have cared less about the former, and as for the latter— well, one or two were tempting, but if they'd been picked up as a series, that would have taken too much of my time. I felt Darcy needed me just then."

"Mother," Darcy quavered, "I wish you'd told me this before. Now I don't know what to do."

"Are you asking my advice?" Ariel's voice was shrill with amazement.

"Yes, I guess I am."

"Well, I never thought I'd see the day! But for once, I'm speechless."

"I'm not," said Yvette. "If I had to choose between advancing my career and my man, Louis would win by a mile."

"I quite agree," said Ariel. "Still, it's a choice Darcy must make for herself."

Having returned the volley to Darcy's court, both women turned to look at her expectantly, awaiting her decision.

"Madame Perrigo," she inquired softly, "what if we were to forget about our contract?"

"Dar-cee!" Yvette exclaimed. "Are you saying what I think you're saying?"

"Yes." Darcy spoke more firmly now. "Yes, I am."

Yvette nodded thoughtfully. "We've only just scratched the surface of the Champagne Blonde campaign. As yet, we've done nothing that can't be reversed fairly easily, and if we put Miles to work on it, he might even come up with a tie-in so we could use the print ads of you as an introduction to the ads featuring Ariel."

"If you played up the family connection," Ariel suggested slyly, "that couldn't help but enhance the St. Denis mystique."

"Yes." Yvette grinned. "That had occurred to me. At any rate, if Dar-cee were to withdraw in favor of you, it would put an entirely new complexion on the situation."

"And I'd be willing to buy back my contract," Darcy added hopefully.

She held up the check, but Yvette only laughed and

shook her head. "That won't be necessary, *ma petite*," she declared fondly. "You're fired!"

"In that case," said Darcy, "since I still haven't had my hot bath, why don't I leave the two of you alone to settle the rest of it."

Neither Ariel nor Yvette tried to stop her as she rose and left the room. She went into the bathroom, turned on the taps, and began getting out of her clothes, her head reeling with the possibility that she might be granted another chance with Jordan.

That night at Santino's when she'd first met him, he had accused her of wanting to prove to herself that she was still desirable. She had adamantly denied it, but in the interim she had learned he was right. And if she'd doubted her desirability then, her doubts were multiplied many times over now.

It wasn't that she questioned her ability to attract a man like Jordan temporarily. About all that was required for a woman to succeed as a one-night stand was a warm and willing body and, oh Lord, she'd been warm and more than willing.

She supposed, to be more precise, it was her lovability she questioned. She was plagued by misgivings as she considered how she might make the most of her reprieve.

Did she dare to hope that the figurehead's resemblance to her was not a coincidence? Should she go to Jordan, tell him she loved him, and offer herself to him for as long as he wanted her?

Every instinct told her directness was the wisest course. Otherwise, he was certainly lost to her. But could she do it?

The answer to that question was a fearful, yet unequivocal no.

There had been a time—before Tim's infidelity—when she could have. In those days she'd been blissfully ignorant. She'd had enough blind faith in herself that she had never seriously entertained the idea that she might be rejected by someone she loved.

Now, however, she knew what she was risking. She had lost her innocence, and she knew that whatever approach she took must leave her some face-saving way out if Jordan didn't return her love. And if the direct approach was no good, what options did that leave? How could she play it—

Play it!

The impact of these two short words hit Darcy like a thunderbolt. They seemed to sear into her mind so that she was paralyzed by them. For the next minute she stared at the water gushing into the tub without moving. Then the germ of an idea blossomed. She turned off the taps and ran into the bedroom.

The garment bag containing the costume for the commercial was lying across the foot of the bed, just as she'd noticed when she had come through to the bathroom, but the script was nowhere in sight.

She lifted the garment bag out of the way, expecting to find the slim buff-colored folder beneath it. When she saw that the folder wasn't there, her eyes made a hasty search of the room. Where was it, she wondered. She felt herself becoming more frantic by the second.

Get a grip on yourself, Darcy, she told herself. Try to keep calm and think.

"I'll ask Yvette where she put it."

She said the words with some determination, and the sound of her voice brought a vestige of control. She had started toward the living room when she caught a glimpse of one corner of the manila folder peeking out from under the bed. Apparently, it had fallen off and skidded under the fringe on the spread.

Now that she'd found the script, Darcy's movements were slow, deliberate. She picked it up and took it with her, hugging it to her chest as she returned to the bathroom. Once there, she closed and locked the door and tossed a handful of bath salts into the water.

She set the folder down long enough to strip off her panties and bra. Then she stepped into the tub, settled

back in the steamy strawberry-scented water, and prepared to study the role she must play.

It didn't take long to read through the few typewritten
pages. Although there were several treatments of the
commercial, it would run only thirty seconds when the
film was edited. The bulk of the script was a description
of the location shots which were to be obtained on board
the *Compass Rose*, with technical directions full of camera angles, pans, zooms, and two shots.

The action was to start with an aerial shot of the boat
sailing and shift to a closeup of the figurehead. Darcy's
face would be superimposed over the lifeless figurehead's, and when her image was the dominant one, the
scene would fade out. In the next scene, the boat was
riding at anchor. It was evening, and she, in her role as
the seagoing Galatea, was cavorting on deck with the
actor who was playing the captain.

There was narration but little dialogue, and her character had no lines. Mostly the role called for her to flit
around looking wraithlike yet sexy.

"Not much help here," Darcy murmured pensively as
she closed the folder. Reaching out one slender, dripping
arm, she put the script out of harm's way on the vanity
before she tucked her hair into a shower cap and lay back
in the tub.

She felt restless, anxious to take some sort of action,
but for the next quarter-hour she forced herself to stay
in the hot, soothing water.

It was some consolation that at least she had a point
of departure. She would get into the figurehead costume
and find the *Compass Rose*. If—please, God—Jordan
loved her even half as much as she loved him, there was
nothing to worry about. And if he didn't—well, then
she would just have to play it by ear.

If worse came to worst, she would try to pass it off
lightly by telling him she'd come there only to give him
a preview of the television commercial.

Chapter 15

THE LAST THING Darcy had expected was that Jordan would not be on board the *Compass Rose*. She sat in the cockpit with her knees drawn up under her chin, trying to stay warm in the dark, chilly night.

The fog had gotten worse. On the waterfront it was so thick that it obscured the lights along the piers. Darcy could see only a faint, milky halo from the one nearest the *Compass Rose*.

She huddled into her raincoat, shivering at the clammy feel of the lining against the bare skin of her shoulders and back. The damp of the fog had soaked into the coat so that it was rapidly becoming useless, and the costume she was wearing underneath it afforded little protection from the cold. There were yards of material in the dress, but it was white chiffon and not terribly substantial.

When she'd tried it on in front of the mirror in her bedroom, she had been pleased with the way she looked.

The costume fastened over one shoulder and fell in graceful folds about her body, swirling about her thighs and clinging to her hips and bosom. The dress was designed so that the thicknesses of chiffon varied, permitting occasional glimpses of creamy skin. More than a hint of the delicate blush of her nipples showed through. It was really quite flattering in the way it revealed enough to entice yet concealed enough to tantalize.

For the commercial it was to have been worn over a flesh-colored body stocking, but considering the nature of her mission, Darcy had dispensed with that. Not that it would have done much to keep her warm on a night such as this.

Thanks to Yvette's directions, she'd found the ketch easily, but so far that was the only thing that had gone according to plan. She had arrived at the *Compass Rose* only to find the boat dark, deserted, and securely locked.

She had tried to get a look at the figurehead, crawling out onto the bowsprit as far as she dared. But because of the darkness and the fog and the way the bow angled back toward the water, without a flashlight she wasn't able to see much.

And a flashlight wasn't the only thing she had forgotten. She hadn't thought to bring her sneakers either, and it hadn't occurred to her that her pumps were not suitable for deck wear until she was preparing to board the boat.

She knew how annoyed Jordan would be if she were to gouge the teakwood deck with her shoes, so she had removed them. At first her bare feet had been cold, but now she had little sensation of any sort in them.

Wondering if there was any danger of being frostbitten in above-freezing temperatures, Darcy tucked her feet beneath her and wrapped the hem of the raincoat around her toes.

Think of something else, she advised herself. Think of seeing Jordan, and you won't notice how cold and damp you are. You'll forget how dark it is, and how still.

When she'd settled down in the cockpit, there had been lights showing in the portholes of some of the other boats. She had heard bits of conversation and, now and again, an outburst of laughter from the neighboring sloop.

Now, however, the sloop, like the *Compass Rose*, was dark. Only the slap of the water against the pier and the lonely hoot of a foghorn disturbed the silence.

It must be very late, she thought. She tried to look at her wristwatch, but it was too dark to read the time.

Where is Jordan, she wondered crossly.

Maybe she should go home and try again tomorrow. She was tired. The molded fiberglass seat in the cockpit was hard and uncomfortable without the cushions, which Jordan must have locked away in the lazarette.

Darcy stretched and shifted about, trying to ease her cramped muscles. At last she drew her knees up again. Wrapping her arms about her legs, she slid her hands inside the sleeves of the raincoat to keep them warm.

I'll count to a thousand, she decided. If Jordan's not here by the time I've finished, I'll leave.

She began counting, spacing the numbers evenly, and before she had reached fifty, her head nodded forward to rest upon her knees and she drifted off to sleep.

"Darcy? Come on, Goldilocks. Snap out of it."

Jordan's voice jolted Darcy awake. Confused, she opened her eyes and stared at his face, so close to hers.

"Wha—? Where—?"

All at once she remembered where she was and why. Aghast that he should have found her this way, she compounded her mistakes by trying to stand up. Her legs were too stiff to support her. Her knees buckled and she staggered and would have fallen if Jordan hadn't caught her. He half dragged, half carried her toward the companionway.

"My God, you're freezing!" he exclaimed. "What in blue blazes were you thinking of?"

"I was waiting for you," she replied.

Her voice wobbled alarmingly, and she realized she was near tears with relief that he'd finally returned. She cleared her throat and blinked in the sudden brightness when he switched on the lights in the galley.

"Where have you been?" she demanded, but Jordan ignored the question.

"Let's get you out of that wet coat," he said.

"No!" She recalled what she was wearing under the raincoat and pushed his hands away from the belt, struggling to escape his hold on her. When he persisted in his attempts to untie the belt, she offered the lame excuse, "I—uh, I'm cold."

"I'm not surprised you're cold," said Jordan. "It's a raw night out. But that coat is so wet, it can't be much help."

"Even so, I'd rather keep it on for a while."

With a negligent shrug Jordan turned away from her and opened one of the lockers, then another and another. "I know I have a bottle of Scotch here somewhere," he muttered. He found the liquor in the next cabinet he tried. As he poured out a generous glassful, he explained, "I've been loading supplies, so things are a little disorganized."

He handed Darcy her drink and poured another for himself. He leaned back against the counter as he drank it.

"How long have you been waiting?" he asked.

She swallowed some of the Scotch before she tried to answer. She coughed because it was so fiery, and felt more awkward and embarrassed than she had before.

"I'm not sure," she replied noncommittally as she consulted her watch. Astonished at how much time had passed, she said, "I think about two hours."

Jordan's eyebrows shot up. "Care to tell me what prompted this unexpected visit?"

"I—uh, that is—" At a loss for words, she averted her face and raised her glass to her lips.

"Perhaps you just happened to be in the neighborhood and you thought you might as well drop in."

She risked a glance at him. The laughter in his eyes convinced her that he must not care for her at all. If he had, he would hardly have found her plight so amusing.

"Very funny," she said miserably. "Not too original, but funny." She set her glass on the counter. "I can see I shouldn't have come here. I think I'd better leave now."

"Not so fast, young lady!" Jordan slammed his own glass down. In two long strides he had stepped around her and was blocking the path to the companionway. "You're not going anywhere till you've told me why you got the sudden urge to see me tonight."

"All right," she retorted sharply. *"All right!"*

His unyielding stance and the hard set of his jaw told her he'd meant every word of his threat. She was left with no alternative but to brazen it out.

"Madame Perrigo told me about the figurehead." Her hands went to the belt of the raincoat. Her fingers were still numb with cold, and she fumbled a bit before she was able to undo the knot. "She said she thought it looked a lot like me, and I came here to ask if you'd take me with you when you leave Seattle." At last the belt was loosened and she quickly slipped out of the coat. "I also wanted to show you this!"

When she revealed the costume, Jordan's eyes widened. She tossed the coat aside and spun around in a hasty pirouette that would allow him to see her from every angle.

"If this is supposed to be a joke," Jordan said harshly, "I fail to see the humor in it."

He hadn't actually raised his voice, but Darcy could feel the icy rage that emanated from him. When she completed her turn, his eyes were narrowed and his mouth was white-rimmed and thinned to a grim line. His contempt struck her as tangibly as if he'd slapped her. She recoiled, backing away from him, bumping into the counter and upsetting the glass of Scotch. An amber pool of liquid spilled out, and the glass rolled onto the deck and shattered.

"Oh, Lord!" she cried, horrified. "I'm so sorry."

Choking back a sob, she knelt to pick up the shards of broken glass.

"Leave it," Jordan ordered.

"No, it's all right," she argued tremulously. "It will only take me a minute to clean this up."

He grasped her by the shoulders, pulled her into his arms, and lifted her away from the counter. Before he released her, he gave her an exasperated shake.

"You little idiot! Don't you know any better than to run around broken glass in your bare feet?"

This time Darcy was unable to smother her sob. Tears filled her eyes. Before she could stop them, they had spilled over and were running down her cheeks. She kept her face lowered, hoping Jordan wouldn't see them, but her efforts were futile.

"Darcy?" He breathed her name softly, with wonderment. "Oh, God, Darcy! It's not a joke, is it?"

The tenderness in his voice caused a new freshet of tears. She could only shake her head in response, but this must have been enough to persuade him, because he tilted her face toward his and began drying the tears with kisses. His lips moved as gently as a sigh over her cheeks, her forehead, her temples, returning again and again to her eyelids.

Then his arms closed around her and she swayed into them. She tipped her head back and sought his mouth with her own, and when she found it she kissed him deeply, passionately, communicating all the love she had kept bottled up inside.

She was so intoxicated by the heady taste of his mouth that she was unaware he'd drawn her out of the galley and along the passageway to his stateroom until he sank down onto the bed. As he lay back against the pillows, one of his arms hooked around her thighs, sweeping her down with him. She landed on top of him and his hands moved over her hips, molding her body to the hot, virile thrust of his.

"You're still cold," he muttered hoarsely.

Darcy buried her face in the hollow of his neck and nodded.

Jordan kissed her hair and adroitly unpinned the shoulder clip that held the costume in place.

"If you want me to, I'll warm you," he whispered.

"What did you have in mind?"

He rolled her over suddenly so that she was covered by the delicious warmth of his body. Resting his forehead against hers, he smiled lazily into her eyes as he said, "I thought we'd rub our bodies together and start a fire."

She replied by tugging at his sweater, and he let go of her so that she could pull it over his head. As she wrapped her arms around his neck to pull him down to her, she murmured breathlessly, "Let's."

His open mouth claimed hers, and she responded wildly, inflamed by the erotic play of his lips and teeth and tongue. She ran her palms along his shoulders and down his neck, rejoicing in his rugged leanness, and when her searching hands moved lower, a ragged groan escaped him.

He rolled away from her to pull off his shoes and socks and strip off the rest of his clothes. Then he was embracing her again. Their mouths met and clung in a long, mesmerizing kiss, while their hands explored and fondled, rediscovering each other and rekindling an explosive rush of desire.

She moaned with the intensity of her pleasure when his lips left hers to sample the hollows at the base of her throat. He followed the arc of her collarbone to the rise of her breasts, trailed a feverish line of kisses along the fragrant valley between them, and finally his tongue flicked over the nipples, teasing them to exquisitely sensitive erectness.

"Oh, Jordan," she gasped. "Oh, darling, I think your remedy is already working."

"I'm glad to hear that, Goldilocks. I can't wait for you much longer."

He whispered the things he wanted to do to her. The enticing suggestions and the husky growl of his voice excited her beyond endurance.

She was desperate with wanting him, and she clutched at his shoulders, letting him know that she couldn't wait either. But before she could say the words aloud, he had parted her thighs with his knee and was arching her toward him with his hands beneath her hips. He moved onto her and around her and into her, deepening his possession of her with hard, sensuous caresses so that it seemed that every part of her body came into contact with some part of his. And then he was deep inside, at the very core of her being, demanding more of her, demanding all of her.

How she welcomed his demands! She gave herself over to them and met them with demands of her own, abandoning herself to the dizzying spiral of delight that carried her to the very pinnacle of ecstasy, utterly losing herself in the fluid shock waves that signaled fulfillment.

"Have you any idea what kind of chances you were taking, running around the public streets in that little bit of cloth you call a costume?"

The way Jordan was holding her, the way he was touching her, belied the sternness of his question. Darcy snuggled closer to him and planted a kiss at the corner of his mouth.

"But I was wearing my raincoat—"

"This time I'm not going to fall for your coaxing, Goldilocks," Jordan declared. "A man can be made a sucker of just so often, and this man is wise to you."

"But, Jordan—"

"I want your solemn promise you won't do it again."

"You have it," she said softly.

"And another thing—"

"What's that?" she asked.

"No more picking up strange men."

"I'll agree to that on the condition you promise not to pick up strange women."

Jordan chuckled. "You're forgetting, Darcy, you weren't a stranger."

"I hadn't really forgotten," she contradicted him delightedly. "I just wanted to be sure you hadn't. You tried to talk about it the other morning. Will you tell me about it now?"

"Gladly, if you're ready to listen."

"Oh, I'll listen," Darcy said with feeling. "And that's another promise!"

"Okay, then."

Before he began, Jordan sat up and switched on the ship's lantern on the nightstand. Darcy held the sheet close to her breasts and sat up beside him. Smiling at her display of modesty, Jordan slipped his arm around her again.

"I suppose I should start with the way my aunt tried to finagle me into meeting you."

"She did that?"

"She did," Jordan affirmed, "but it was years ago, before I'd mellowed to the point of humoring her whims— so I just dug in my heels. At the time I was in no position to think of marriage anyway, and eventually she got behind another candidate."

"You said you'd come to my wedding," Darcy remarked.

"That's right, and when I saw you that day, I could have kicked myself for not going along with Aunt Jenny's attempts to get us together." Jordan's arm tightened possessively about her. His voice was rough with torment as he went on, "I watched you walking down the aisle to marry another man, and it was pure torture! I couldn't understand my reaction till later, but when the minister came to the part of the service where he called on anyone who knew of a reason why the marriage shouldn't take place to speak out, I had this crazy impulse to shout that I did. I wanted to say it was all a mistake, because you were meant for me."

"I wish you had," Darcy murmured.

"Nonsense," Jordan exclaimed gruffly. "You'd have laughed me out of the church—or had me clapped into a straitjacket!"

"I'm not so sure about that. I might have agreed with you. As Marlowe wrote, 'Who ever loved that loved not at first sight?'"

"So he did, but someone else wrote, 'Never seek to tell thy love,' so instead of speaking out, I kept quiet. I figured it just wasn't in the cards for us. I tried to put you out of my mind, but I couldn't, not entirely. Then when I heard you'd separated from Cummins, I approached your mother. I thought I was pretty damned discreet, but she tumbled to the fact that my questions about you were prompted by something more than casual interest, and once I'd taken her into my confidence, she told me a lot about you."

"Such as?"

"Well, the first time I spoke to her about you was shortly after you'd filed for divorce, and she told me quite frankly that you weren't ready to get involved with anyone just then. She advised me to bide my time—said she'd let me know when she thought you were ready."

"Then that night at Santino's—"

"Ariel told me you planned on going there," said Jordan. "She was afraid I'd jump the gun, but by then she knew I *had* to see you again."

"No wonder you knew so much about me! And you led me to believe you'd read it all in my face."

"Well, Darcy, your face *is* expressive—" Jordan grinned indulgently—"but not *that* expressive."

"You'll never know how glad I am to hear that," she cried relievedly.

"Amen," said Jordan. "Anyway, when I saw you, I couldn't resist sending the drink to your table." A rueful smile touched the corners of his mouth. "When you accepted the drink and left the restaurant with me, I didn't know whether to kiss you or spank you."

"You were angry?"

"Damned right I was," Jordan answered sharply. Then he smiled again, not at all bitterly this time, and said, "But that didn't stop me from wanting you. I wanted you so much, it hurt. When you changed your mind at the last minute, I decided I'd waited as long as I could. I phoned Ariel later that night and we had a long talk about you—"

"And she did her bit by setting me up for the weekend," Darcy supplied.

"Yes, but only because I insisted on it."

"I seem to recall your telling me you had no idea I'd be at Roche Harbor."

Jordan laughed. "I can see I'll have to be on my toes with you, Goldilocks, but I'd like to point out that I didn't actually lie to you. What I said was, Aunt Jenny had given other reasons for inviting me. I didn't like misleading you, but Ariel had warned me you were still wary about entering into a relationship. She told me you withdrew the minute a guy came on too strong, so I tried to play it cool. Except that I couldn't seem to stop myself from propositioning you every time we were alone. And besides—oh hell, Darcy! I'm no good at making flowery speeches."

"So I've noticed," Darcy laughingly complained. "I don't mind telling you, after having grown up surrounded by people who call everybody darling, you were quite a novelty. I didn't know what to make of a man who said I was a good kid one minute and tried to get me to go to bed with him the next."

"You seem to have borne up nicely though."

"And I'll continue to as long as you keep on holding me this way."

Grinning at her rejoinder, Jordan folded her closer and Darcy melted languidly into his arms.

"You've admitted you have a tough time paying compliments, but how are you at accepting them?"

"Not much better," he confessed dryly.

"In that case I won't tell you how much I love you."

For a moment Jordan looked startled. Then he realized she was teasing. One of his hands swept upward from her waist to cup the rich weight of her breast while the other wandered slowly, in a long delicious caress, across her belly to her thighs.

"If you play your cards right, I think I could learn to like that particular compliment."

"You seem to be taking it well," she purred, "so I think I'll tell you—"

Jordan stopped her with a kiss. His mouth still hovered over hers as he whispered, "If you've no objection, Goldilocks, right about now I'd rather you *showed* me."

Chapter **16**

THE FOG WAS even thicker the following morning, which meant the marina was relatively quiet. Darcy awoke before Jordan. She stayed in bed for a while, alternately dozing and glorying in the luxury of waking up to find herself sheltered by the warmth of his body.

Even on this gray day, she decided, the stateroom was very cozy and welcoming. When she had showered and found her way to the galley, she decided it was wonderful, too. As the boat rose and fell on the wake of a passing trawler, she fancied that being in the cabin of the *Compass Rose* was like being rocked in loving arms.

She heard Jordan stirring about and the shower running, and hurried to start breakfast. When Jordan came out of the stateroom, he found her dressed in one of his shirts, happily putting the finishing touches on the table in the dinette.

He kissed her good morning and ruffled her hair. "Do I smell bacon?" he asked.

"You do." She smiled. "Sit down and I'll bring our plates."

"You'll spoil me," he warned.

"I want to. Maybe then you'll agree to give me a trial at crewing for you." She dropped a kiss on the top of his head as she set his plate in front of him. "I hope you like your eggs scrambled."

"They're perfect," he called after her in an imitation of Miles Brucker as she left the dinette. "Absolutely perfect."

She returned with the coffee pot, filled their cups, and sat down opposite him. She was unfolding her napkin when she glanced up at Jordan and saw that he was completely absorbed with watching her.

"Is something wrong?" she asked. He looked distressingly solemn.

"Did you have any trouble with the stove?"

"No."

"That's amazing," he said. "I haven't been able to get it to work properly for several weeks now, so I ordered a new one."

"Well, it's all in the way you prime it."

Jordan's scrutiny of her continued. "You cleaned up the broken glass," he said accusingly.

"I—uh, I put on my shoes," Darcy replied, "but only long enough to do the job, and I was very careful not to mark the deck."

"The hell with the deck," Jordan said flatly. "It's your feet I was concerned about."

For a few minutes they concentrated on their breakfasts. Then, in the same uninflected tone, Jordan said, "You're a good cook, Goldilocks."

"It's only bacon and eggs," she replied hesitantly, "but thank you."

"You look great in my shirt, too," he added.

Darcy turned away from him. Faced with his less than

enthusiastic response, she felt increasingly uneasy.

"Look," she said stiffly, "I apologize if this is too much domesticity for you. I didn't mean to pressure you—"

"No, Darcy." Jordan reached across the table to cover her hand with his. "I'm the one who should apologize. Don't think I'm not enjoying all this, because I am. I've dreamed about having you here with me for so long, I can't begin to tell you how much it means to me that you're actually here. The trouble is, I can't help wondering how long it's going to last."

"But, Jordan, last night I asked if you'd take me with you when you leave Seattle, and not ten minutes ago I told you I'd like to sign on as your crew."

"What about your modeling?" he asked quietly.

"Oh, that." Darcy shrugged dismissively. "Didn't I mention that I've been fired?"

"Fired!" Jordan sounded outraged. "But why? You were fantastic yesterday."

"I appreciate the compliment, especially coming from you, but even before I went into the job, I knew that modeling wasn't my cup of tea. Fortunately, Yvette agrees with me because, as it turns out, my mother is eager to become the spokeswoman for Perrigo Wines."

"So they're switching to Ariel!"

Was there a hint of jubilation in Jordan's voice? Darcy glanced at him curiously and saw that he was grinning.

"I don't understand you," she said. "First you seemed offended because I've been dumped in favor of my mother, and now you look as if you're pleased about it."

"Only because it means you were serious when you offered to crew for me."

"Well of course I'm serious. Do you think I make a habit of going from man to man, offering my services as cook and bottlewasher and—Jordan, exactly what does a 'crew' do?"

"Oh, Goldilocks, that's something I can't wait to begin teaching you." He jumped to his feet and tugged at her hand, urging her up beside him. "I can't believe it!" He shouted with laughter and swung her around elatedly. "I'd about given up hope that there would ever be a future for us. When you agreed to the modeling job, I moved up the departure date for my trip. I guess the cruise was my equivalent to the way men used to join the Foreign Legion when they were disappointed in love. Last night I was at the end of my rope. I waited outside your apartment building for you to come home, and I was so desperate that I was prepared to carry you off by force if I had to, and now you're here and you're really coming with me!"

Jordan's confession made her smile so hard that her face hurt. She realized she must look foolish, but Jordan didn't seem to notice. He was hugging her as if he'd never let her go and raining a flurry of kisses on her face. In return, she hugged and kissed him, and before long they were so wrapped up in celebrating each other, they lost track of everything else.

Epilogue

ON A FINE sunny morning a week later, the *Compass Rose* slipped away from its berth in Shilshole Bay and headed north, bound for the Strait of Juan de Fuca and the Pacific.

It had been another hectic week. Jordan had been busy loading supplies while Darcy had her hands full arranging to sublet her apartment and putting her furniture into storage.

Jordan was teaching her celestial navigation, too. Just last night she'd taken her sightings, done her calculations, and proudly announced that she'd gotten an accurate fix on their longitude. She still had some trouble with latitude. In fact, according to her figures they should have been somewhere in the vicinity of Spokane, but Jordan had told her the latitude would come with a little more practice. "And as of tomorrow, you'll have plenty of time to practice," he'd said.

He had gone below to open the champagne shortly after that, but she had remained on deck long enough to say good night to the figurehead.

The sculpted wooden figure bore a striking resemblance to her. She saw a number of similarities, not only in the facial features, but in the torso as well. Beneath the finely carved folds of its Grecian tunic, the slope of the shoulders, the shape of the breasts, the curves of the waist and hips, were remarkably like her own.

When she had first seen the figurehead, she'd marveled that Jordan could have known so much about her body before he'd seen her naked. But if the likeness was a source of bemusement, it was also concrete evidence of his love.

Now, as she sat beside Jordan in the cockpit of the ketch, she felt a deep and abiding contentment.

"Well, Goldilocks," Jordan said softly, "here we are, alone at last."

"Thank God!" She turned her laughing face toward his, but her throat constricted with concern when she saw his watchful expression.

"Are you sure you won't regret this?" he asked. "You know it's not too late to change our plans."

"No." She shook her head emphatically. "Oh, darling, don't you know how much I want to do this? Can't you see how happy I am to be here with you?"

For a few moments Jordan studied her soberly. "All right," he said at last, "but I want you to promise you'll tell me if you decide you've had enough. Just say the word, and we'll head for the nearest port and hop the first plane home."

"I promise," she said with as much solemnity as she could manage. And if the need arose, she would keep that promise. She had learned how essential it was to be honest—to be herself. Thinking of this, it was hard to keep from smiling, and she was relieved to see the incandescent grin that spread across Jordan's face.

"You really enjoy sailing, don't you? Even if it means you'll never get to see yourself on billboards or TV."

"That," she replied, "is a loss I can survive very nicely."

"But won't you miss all the conveniences of the city?"

"Not as long as I have you."

"Sure you won't miss wearing furs and jewelry?" He flashed her a wicked grin.

"The furs I can sacrifice," she returned his teasing. "The jewelry, though—" Darcy paused and brushed back the stubborn lock of hair that had fallen over his forehead. "Well," she went on, "I do adore jewelry!"

Jordan threw his head back and laughed. When he sobered, he lifted her hand to his mouth and kissed each finger. As he touched his lips to the wide gold band he'd given her, he said, "For the time being I'm afraid you'll have to settle for your wedding ring."

"My darling, I'll settle for it forever."

"Forever."

The warm timbre of Jordan's voice as he repeated her vow made her heart sing with anticipation.

"Just think of it!" she cried. "All the glorious days alone. Just the two of us and the sun and the sea—"

"All *I* can think of is the nights!" His blue eyes glinted roguishly as he lounged back against the cushions, and when his arm went around her, she slid closer to him. "By the way," he said, "you never did tell me what was in that last-minute wedding gift Ariel brought to the church yesterday."

Darcy's face was rosy as she replied, "That wasn't a gift. It was a not too subtle hint."

"It looked like a book."

"It was a book," she admitted, giving him a look that said "here we go again." "It was Dr. Spock's *Baby and Child Care.*"

A smile lurked in Jordan's eyes and played around the corners of his lips. "Would you believe Aunt Jenny gave *me* a copy?"

"Yes, I'd believe it!"

Her tone of voice was so impassioned that both of them burst out laughing.

"We'll have to see what we can do about that," said Jordan. Bending his head close to hers, he kissed her ear and whispered, "But not just yet. For the next year or so I want you all to myself."

Darcy nodded agreement and pressed her cheek to his.

As they sailed farther out into the Sound, the breeze freshened. The sun moved higher and the skyline of the city faded away behind the stern of the *Compass Rose*. Eventually, even the snow-capped peak of Mt. Rainier disappeared, but Darcy didn't notice. She was too enchanted with the hint of rainbows in the spray that sometimes drifted over the bow of the ketch.

After a while, she shifted slightly, nestling into the curve of Jordan's arm so that her head rested on his shoulder. She savored the sense of belonging the gesture gave her.

After Tim had left, she had allowed herself to drift from day to day, rudderless and without purpose. Then Jordan had come into her life and, with his rough magnetism, he'd shown her what she wanted—what she needed.

Someday soon she wanted to have a child—Jordan's child. Maybe they would have a little boy who looked like his father. Jordan's son would probably be strong-willed and something of a daredevil. When he was hurt she would put Band-Aids on his scrapes and kiss away his tears. He would bring her caterpillars and bunches of wildflowers, and sometimes he would ask her to read him bedtime stories.

Or perhaps they would have a little girl. Naturally, Jordan's daughter would idolize her daddy. She'd be bright and sunny and clever, and she'd have her father's directness. When she was four or so, she'd swear she was going to be a nurse, a fireman, *and* a ballerina when she grew up, and with a father like Jordan, maybe she would.

Or then again, perhaps they would have two children. A son and a daughter would be ideal.

But she wanted more than children. She wanted to be generous and loving and full of life and open to adventure. She wanted to value each moment of the day for whatever it might bring. But most of all, she wanted Jordan, because without him, none of this would be worth having.

Jordan had done more than share his dreams with her. He'd made her an integral part of them. He was her lodestone, her compass rose.

WATCH FOR
6 NEW TITLES EVERY MONTH!

Second Chance at Love

_____ 06195-6 **SHAMROCK SEASON #35** Jennifer Rose

_____ 06304-5 **HOLD FAST TIL MORNING #36** Beth Brookes

_____ 06282-0 **HEARTLAND #37** Lynn Fairfax

_____ 06408-4 **FROM THIS DAY FORWARD #38** Jolene Adams

_____ 05968-4 **THE WIDOW OF BATH #39** Anne Devon

_____ 06400-9 **CACTUS ROSE #40** Zandra Colt

_____ 06401-7 **PRIMITIVE SPLENDOR #41** Katherine Swinford

_____ 06424-6 **GARDEN OF SILVERY DELIGHTS #42** Sharon Francis

_____ 06521-8 **STRANGE POSSESSION #43** Johanna Phillips

_____ 06326-6 **CRESCENDO #44** Melinda Harris

_____ 05818-1 **INTRIGUING LADY #45** Daphne Woodward

_____ 06547-1 **RUNAWAY LOVE #46** Jasmine Craig

_____ 06423-8 **BITTERSWEET REVENGE #47** Kelly Adams

_____ 06541-2 **STARBURST #48** Tess Ewing

_____ 06540-4 **FROM THE TORRID PAST #49** Ann Cristy

_____ 06544-7 **RECKLESS LONGING #50** Daisy Logan

_____ 05851-3 **LOVE'S MASQUERADE #51** Lillian Marsh

_____ 06148-4 **THE STEELE HEART #52** Jocelyn Day

_____ 06422-X **UNTAMED DESIRE #53** Beth Brookes

_____ 06651-6 **VENUS RISING #54** Michelle Roland

_____ 06595-1 **SWEET VICTORY #55** Jena Hunt

_____ 06575-7 **TOO NEAR THE SUN #56** Aimee Duvall

_____ 05625-1 **MOURNING BRIDE #57** Lucia Curzon

_____ 06411-4 **THE GOLDEN TOUCH #58** Robin James

_____ 06596-X **EMBRACED BY DESTINY #59** Simone Hadary

_____ 06660-5 **TORN ASUNDER #60** Ann Cristy

_____ 06573-0 **MIRAGE #61** Margie Michaels

_____ 06650-8 **ON WINGS OF MAGIC #62** Susanna Collins

All of the above titles are $1.75 per copy

Available at your local bookstore or return this form to:

SECOND CHANCE AT LOVE
Book Mailing Service, P.O. Box 690, Rockville Cntr., NY 11570

Please send me the titles checked above. I enclose _____.
Include 75¢ for postage and handling if one book is ordered; 50¢ per book for
two to five. If six or more are ordered, postage is free. California, Illinois, New
York and Tennessee residents please add sales tax.

NAME _____

ADDRESS _____

CITY_____ STATE/ZIP_____

Allow six weeks for delivery.   SK-41

WHAT READERS SAY ABOUT
SECOND CHANCE AT LOVE BOOKS

"Your books are the greatest!"
—*M. N., Carteret, New Jersey**

"I have been reading romance novels for quite some time, but the SECOND CHANCE AT LOVE books are the most enjoyable."
—*P. R., Vicksburg, Mississippi**

"I enjoy SECOND CHANCE [AT LOVE] more than any books that I have read and I do read a lot."
—*J. R., Gretna, Louisiana**

"For years I've had my subscription in to Harlequin. Currently there is a series called Circle of Love, but you have them all beat."
—*C. B., Chicago, Illinois**

"I really think your books are exceptional...I read Harlequin and Silhouette and although I still like them, I'll buy your books over theirs. SECOND CHANCE [AT LOVE] is more interesting and holds your attention and imagination with a better story line..."
—*J. W., Flagstaff, Arizona**

"I've read many romances, but yours take the 'cake'!"
—*D. H., Bloomsburg, Pennsylvania**

"Have waited ten years for *good* romance books. Now I have them."
—*M. P., Jacksonville, Florida**

*Names and addresses available upon request